COOPER'S CORNER CHRONICLE

Twin Celebrations Planned for This Weekend

Cooper's Corner residents have always known that our little town in the Berkshires is the closest you can get to paradise, and this weekend we'll be gathering once again to celebrate our founding father, Theodore Cooper. The Founder's Day barbecue promises to attract residents and tourists alike, and what a feast they'll find. Ed Taylor's back with his lip-smacking barbecued chicken, and Tubb's Café has been whipping up potato salad and coleslaw by the bucket. There'll be balloons, rock climbing and pony rides for the kids, and a live band for everybody to enjoy.

What makes this year's event extra special is the opening of Twin Oaks Bed and Breakfast. The brother-and-sister team of Clint and Maureen Cooper have converted the family homestead into a dream destination for weary city folks and romantic lovers. Cozy eiderdown quilts and four-poster beds, pine furniture, fresh flowers and Clint's country breakfast buffet offer the hospitality New England is renowned for.

And though she is being discreet, Maureen is hinting that one of the guests this weekend just might end up putting Cooper's Corner on the map....

D0377041

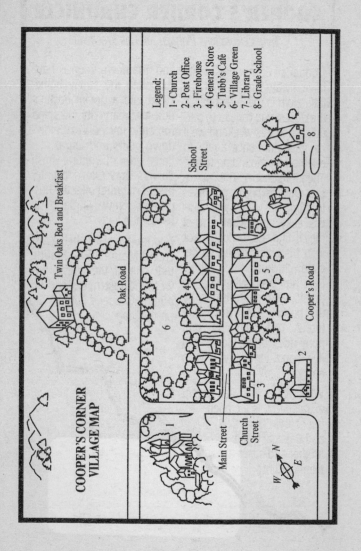

COOPER'S CORNER

TARA TAYLOR QUINN

His Brother's Bride

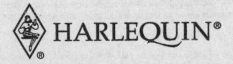

HARLEQUIN®

TORONTO • NEW YORK • LONDON
AMSTERDAM • PARIS • SYDNEY • HAMBURG
STOCKHOLM • ATHENS • TOKYO • MILAN • MADRID
PRAGUE • WARSAW • BUDAPEST • AUCKLAND

For Marsha Zinberg
Who not only took pity on a slightly pathetic, unpublished dreamer, but believed in my right to that dream, spent years teaching me, and finally bought my first book. Feels as if we've come full circle, yet I'm still just as excited with each new project we do as I was with the first. I'm incredibly thankful for the honor of knowing you.

 HARLEQUIN BOOKS
225 Duncan Mill Road, Don Mills,
Ontario, Canada M3B 3K9

ISBN-13: 978-0-373-61252-9
ISBN-10: 0-373-61252-4

HIS BROTHER'S BRIDE

Tara Taylor Quinn is acknowledged as the author of this work.

Visit us at www.eHarlequin.com

Printed in U.S.A.

Dear Reader,

Welcome to Cooper's Corner. Once you meet the people here, stay at the new Twin Oaks Bed and Breakfast, taste Clint's griddle cakes, play with Maureen's three-year-old twin girls and sit down to have a man-to-man talk with twelve-year-old Keegan, you're going to understand why I left part of my heart here.

Cooper's Corner is a blend of New England class, breathtaking Berkshire beauty and small-town charm. It's the kind of place I think of when I'm feeling overwhelmed by life and have to believe there really is a world where people love and care for each other above all else, where the pace is slow and where values matter more than advancement.

And one of the great things about Twin Oaks is that it's specifically designed for people like us who don't live in Cooper's Corner but want to be a member of the family anyway. It's for city folks who need to be reminded what matters, a place where busy people can find moments of peace and warmth and love. A place where families go to spend time together, play parlor games or take long hikes. You'll see as you spend the year with us that Twin Oaks is for everyone, no matter what age, gender or stage in life. It's all here.

So sit back, allow the peace to wash over you and...

Get ready to fall in love.

Tara Taylor Quinn

I love to hear from readers:
P.O. Box 15065
Scottsdale, AZ 85267
www.tarataylorquinn.com

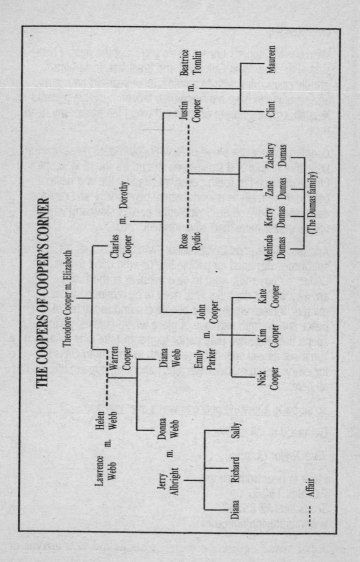

THE COOPERS OF COOPER'S CORNER

Theodore Cooper m. Elizabeth

Warren Cooper

Charles Cooper m. Dorothy

Justin Cooper m. Beatrice Tomlin

Lawrence Webb m. Helen Webb

Donna Webb

Diana Webb

John Cooper m. Emily Parker

Rose Rydic

Jerry Albright m. Sally

Diana   Richard

Nick Cooper   Kim Cooper   Kate Cooper

Clint   Maureen

Melinda Dumas   Kerry Dumas   Zane Dumas   Zachary Dumas

(The Dumas family)

----- Affair

CHAPTER ONE

SHE SHOULDN'T HAVE COME. The determination that had driven her to return to Cooper's Corner that Founders Day weekend seemed to have deserted her. Or perhaps it had been overshadowed by emotions much more powerful than determination.

Three hours on the road up from Manhattan, Highway 8 had merged into Highway 7, and the lush beauty of the Berkshires surrounded her. Rolling green hills and towering trees—it was a beauty she'd almost forgotten. Or perhaps she had buried it deep inside of her with other things she'd been unable to bear losing. Yet, it would always be a part of her.

Elation at coming home was mixed with a devastation she couldn't endure. Everything was rushing at her too quickly, overpowering her until she could hardly breathe.

Oh, Paul. It hurts so badly.

Cooper's Corner was just ahead.

It had been three and a half years.

She was healing.

Glancing at herself in her rearview mirror, forcing herself to face the gray eyes staring back at her, Laurel London couldn't run from the truth.

Coming home had been a bad idea.

THREE OF THE FOUR GUESTS had checked in. Maureen Cooper wasn't so much worried about the late arrival of the fourth as she was antsy to know that the woman would show up—that opening day was indeed going to be the success she and her brother, Clint, had envisioned in all of their best dreams.

Careful not to drip water on the off-white slacks and light green blouse she'd changed into to welcome her guests, Maureen finished arranging the flowers she'd brought in from the greenhouse, her long chestnut hair uncommonly free and falling around her shoulders as she worked. All of the vases in the guest rooms were full. This one in the gathering room was the last.

It was late August, less than a year since she and Clint had made the final move from their former lives to become proprietors of Twin Oaks Bed and Breakfast. The decision to open during Cooper's Corner Founders Day celebration was a good one. Ready-made festivities awaited their guests in town the next day. A barbecue. Fireworks.

Small-town revelry.

That revelry was what Twin Oaks boasted about most. She and Clint were hoping to cater to New Yorkers and Bostonites: big-city families with children longing for fresh air and wide-open spaces; parents visiting their sons and daughters at Williams College or the Massachusetts College of Liberal Arts, both just a few miles away; honeymooners seeking a romantic hideaway. Twin Oaks would give them a taste of small-town pleasures. There were no fax lines, no Jacuzzi tubs—what Twin Oaks offered was a peaceful respite in the lovely Berkshires.

Tucking in a couple of daisies, Maureen stepped back to assess the results, still listening for the late arrival.

Admittedly, a bit of her nervousness had to do with the guest she'd just shown upstairs a short while before. William Byrd, author of *New England's Best Bed and Break-*

fasts. His book was the bible for travelers looking for just the right place to stay. And he'd mentioned when he'd called to reserve their last remaining room for the grand opening that he was getting ready to put out his next edition.

Of course, the lock on their best guest room had to be the one that was still sticking. Not that he'd seemed to mind. Maureen had offered him another room, but he'd understood that there were always little glitches in any big renovation. He'd been quite effusive in his praise of the house.

And if he included Twin Oaks in his upcoming book, their new and somewhat risky venture would gain the exposure it needed to ensure success....

"Mommy, can we..."

"...have a cookie?"

Maureen turned as her three-year-old angels, dressed in identical denim overall shorts and high-top tennis shoes, came barreling into the gigantic gathering room—the heart of Twin Oaks with its great stone hearth and vintage piano.

Her daughters were this generation's contribution to the forest of trees lining the front drive. The Coopers were known for producing matching pairs, and each time a new set of twins was born, the family would plant a pair of oak trees on either side of the drive to commemorate the event.

Randi and Robin raced toward her, tripping over their feet, their blue-green eyes alight with anticipation.

"Uncle Clint's..."

"...baking cookies."

Light chestnut wisps curling around cherubic faces, the twins skidded to a stop in front of Maureen. Robin grabbed her mother's little finger, Randi her thumb on the opposite hand.

"Please?" they asked together.

Maureen hid a smile. "If Uncle Clint is baking, then you can each have one cookie," she said, stressing the *one*. The girls both had a sweet tooth, and she knew she had to set a limit or they would wangle the whole tray from their uncle.

"Yeah!" The little girls bounced up and down, still holding on to her fingers.

"Just one!" Maureen reminded. "Show Mommy how many one is."

The little girls looked at each other, then held up their pudgy pointer fingers.

"Okay," Maureen said, taking hold of both fingers at once. "You keep them just like this and tell Uncle Clint this is all you can have. Promise?"

The three-year-olds nodded as solemnly as if they held a life in the balance. Then, their fingers stretched out in front of them, they marched purposely from the room.

They were the reason Maureen anxiously awaited her fourth—and tardy—guest. A former detective with the New York City Police Department, Maureen could weather just about anything. But her babies' futures were at stake here. Twin Oaks was more than just an opportunity for her and her brother, Clint, to move their children home to Cooper's Corner. More than a means to support their kids. It was a way to hide Randi and Robin. And herself, too. It was a way to keep them safe. She didn't want anything to go wrong this opening weekend.

Maureen was so lost in thoughts of the past—the trial of New York mobster and murderer Carl Nevil; the threat against her life; the release of Carl's brother Owen from prison; the ensuing "accidents" that were certainly proof of Carl Nevil's threats being fulfilled—that she missed the Lexus pulling into the drive.

But she heard the car door shut and saw the slender woman climb out. Her lemon-blond hair was an unusual but beautiful shade, and she wore it shoulder length and pushed back behind one ear. She looked to be about the same height as Keegan, Clint's twelve-year-old son, who was still inches short of Maureen's own five-eleven frame. The woman was dressed casually, albeit elegantly, in designer jeans and a short-sleeved black sweater that fit her snugly and moved as sleekly as any fine silk should.

"Hi, you must be Laurel." Maureen greeted the woman at the door before her guest could even get up the front steps.

Cool it, Cooper, she admonished herself, *no need to be overeager and make your guests uncomfortable—or worse, suspicious of just how much you have resting on this deal.*

"Yes, I'm Laurel London," the other woman said. Her look was forthright, her handshake strong, yet Maureen sensed an odd kind of detachment in her. "I'm sorry I'm late. I, uh, had to stop…on the way in."

"No problem," Maureen assured her. "Afternoon tea has already been served, I'm afraid, but if you're hungry I'm sure I can get Clint to put something together for you."

"That's okay." Laurel shook her head and looked around. "This place is great," she said softly.

And for a moment, as she was taking in the carefully arranged surroundings, Laurel London seemed to relax— to let down the guarded detachment she'd shown since arriving.

Maureen was glad to see the effect the room was having on her reticent guest. Letting out a silent sigh of relief, she relaxed a bit, too. Twin Oaks was doing just what she and Clint had designed it to do.

She ran a mental check over the guest list. Joining them for the grand opening were a New York University professor and his wife, a single father with school-aged children, William Byrd, of course, and Laurel London. So far they seemed a great group. Easy to please.

Everything was going to be okay.

"What brings you to Twin Oaks?" she asked with real interest as she walked Laurel over to the desk to sign in.

"Just wanted to visit."

"Have you ever been to Cooper's Corner?" Named for Maureen's ancestor, Theodore Cooper, the town attracted many tourists every year.

"I used to live here when I was younger."

"So did I," Maureen said in surprise, looking up from the computer. Laurel appeared to be close to her own thirty-three years. "I was born and lived here until I was seven, and then moved to New York when my father took a teaching job at New York University. My brother, Clint, and I just relocated here a little less than a year ago when our great-uncle left us this place after his death."

Laurel took another lingering—almost yearning?—glance around. "You're lucky. I take it you're related to the Theodore Cooper we all learned about when we studied local history in school?"

"Yeah."

"He was a farmer, right?"

"Among other things." Maureen experienced a surge of a pride she'd forgotten during her years in the city. "He first farmed the area in 1809, and generations of Coopers followed in his footsteps. We turned out to be good at raising cattle. And fruits and vegetables, too."

"And twins, if I'm remembering correctly," Laurel

added. "The Coopers are pretty famous for the number of twins in the family—at least one set every generation, right?" she looked questioningly at Maureen. "So are you a twin?"

Maureen shook her head. "No, but I'm the mother of twins."

The two women chatted for a moment about Randi and Robin, and Laurel's eyes softened as Maureen related a couple of the twins' most recent antics.

"So if your family was so good at farming, why aren't you still at it?" Laurel asked. She seemed in no hurry to get up to her room.

Resting her arms on top of the computer monitor, Maureen explained. "My great-uncle Warren started out as a farmer, but he broke his leg. It was improperly set, which left him with a short leg and pronounced limp, and when he realized he couldn't do farm work any longer, he switched to newspaper writing."

"I remember he owned the local paper when I was in high school."

"He owned it until he retired just a few years ago." Maureen straightened. "So, do you think maybe we knew each other as kids? There couldn't have been more than one first-grade class."

Laurel shook her head. "I didn't move here until I was in high school."

"Your parents relocated?"

"I was placed with a foster family here."

"Oh. I'm sorry." Maureen ripped a form out of the printer and slid it across the desk for Laurel to sign.

"Don't be," the other woman said, scrawling an almost illegible signature across the dotted line. "Those were the happiest years of my life."

The expression on Laurel's face didn't support her

words. Maureen, always the detective, suspected that the blank look was hiding a good amount of pain. Pain that had its roots in Cooper's Corner?

"How long has it been since you've been back?" Maureen asked, filling in the old-fashioned ledger next to the computer.

"Three and a half years." There was no doubting the bone-deep sadness emanating from the other woman at those words.

"So you must know everyone in town pretty well."

"Not really." Laurel shook her head, standing almost perfectly still in front of the desk. "The family I lived with moved away years ago. I left for college right out of high school and haven't been back except for visits since then. A lot has changed."

Maureen supposed it had. And yet, in some ways, Cooper's Corner never seemed to change. It was what she loved most about the place.

"I noticed you're from New York," Maureen said now, giving Laurel her copy of the form she'd signed.

"Uh-huh. Manhattan."

"What do you do there?"

"I'm a television news reporter."

"Really?" Maureen tensed.

A New York reporter? Was this more than just the nostalgic visit Laurel had claimed? What did Laurel London know? Had someone sent her?

If the media had figured out who Maureen was, *where* she was...

If they were planning to air that information...

Laurel was nodding, her face momentarily stress-free as she smiled and named the network for which she worked. A major network.

So why hadn't Maureen recognized her? She'd become

intimately acquainted—at least by sight—with almost all of New York's television news personnel. While there'd been times the reporters and NYPD had been able to support each other on the job, there'd seemed to be as many or more when they'd been at cross-purposes.

Damn. Was she not even going to be able to escape that old life long enough for their opening weekend? She'd had such hopes for this move.

"You obviously like your job," she said, keeping her tone as neutrally friendly as it had been. Keeping up a facade was something Maureen could do while unconscious.

"I do," Laurel slid her folded receipt into the straw purse on her shoulder. "Though I've really only been on the air for the past six months. The last two and a half years I've been working my way up."

Which would explain why Maureen didn't recognize her.

It didn't, however, make the woman any less suspect.

"You're in room four," Maureen said, handing Laurel the big brass key that would unlock the door. "I'll take you up now."

Declining help with her bag, Laurel hoisted the leather satchel over her shoulder and followed Maureen.

"You saw that the front porch looks down the hill over the village," Maureen recited as they climbed the stairs to the guest rooms. "There's a large deck out back that overlooks the flower and vegetable gardens, and there's an open meadow behind if you care to do any reading or lazing in the sun. And if you're feeling more energetic than that, there are steeper hills farther back that have some great bicycle trails...."

By the time Maureen had told Laurel about the buffet breakfast served every morning in the dining room, including walnut griddle cakes that were Clint's specialty, and reminded her that afternoon tea was served in the gathering room she'd just left, they'd reached Laurel's door.

"This is lovely!" the reporter said. Maureen's gaze swept the room with a practiced eye, taking in the casual country décor and the queen-size four-poster pine bed covered with a colorful handmade quilt. A tin of Clint's freshly baked chocolate chip cookies were on the night-stand, alongside the fresh bouquet of flowers she'd left there. An antique bureau stood along one wall, and there was room in the corner alcove for a couple of roll-away beds. Laurel's room was also one of the two with a fireplace.

"You've got a view of the meadow," Maureen said, loath to leave without more information, though the other woman was certainly not encouraging her to linger.

Dropping her satchel on the bed, Laurel moved over to the window. "I'd forgotten how beautiful it all is," she said softly, almost as though speaking to herself.

"Don't see much of this in the city," Maureen agreed. Why was the woman really here?

"No, you sure don't." Laurel turned, her expression distant. "But there's the theater in the city."

"And a job you love."

"There is that."

"So—" Maureen leaned against the doorjamb "—you have someone in particular you're visiting here?"

A woman alone at a B and B. It was hardly unheard-of, but it made Maureen uneasy. Especially when the woman was as beautiful as Laurel London.

So, was she there on a job? Was that why she'd come to Cooper's Corner by herself?

Maureen had to know.

"No. There's no one here I'm planning to see." Laurel's eyes were shadowed again. "More like putting ghosts to rest, I hope."

"Ghosts here in Cooper's Corner?"

"Yeah. The last time I was here…three and a half years ago…I ended up running away. I'm ready to resolve that part of my past so I can get on with the rest of my life."

Maureen sensed that the other woman needed to talk—even if to a stranger. She felt strangely compelled to listen, and only partly to reassure herself that Laurel's appearance in Cooper's Corner had nothing to do with Maureen's own past.

"Does this have to do with a man?" When a woman ran, it usually did.

"Yeah."

"A broken love affair?"

"In a way." Laurel's eyes darkened, and then grew blank.

Funny, Maureen thought, she'd fled New York to find sanctuary in Cooper's Corner, while Laurel had apparently done the exact reverse.

"Is he still around here?" Maureen asked, hoping she wasn't overstepping.

"No." And then, turning back to the window, Laurel said softly, "He's dead."

Oh.

Maureen's heart lurched, her suspicions almost forgotten. "I'm so sorry."

"Don't be." Laurel turned, a sad smile on her face. "You had no way of knowing."

"Still, I shouldn't have pried…."

"No, it's okay. It's probably good to have someone else here know. Might keep me from getting too maudlin."

Holding the other woman's gaze for a moment, Maureen wanted so badly to say something that could ease the pain she read there.

Laurel was beautiful, her blond hair glowing around her, and those dove-gray eyes unusual enough to command a second look. Beautiful—and unmistakably sad.

A dim sheen of tears in her eyes, Laurel was the first to look away.

"You know," Maureen said quickly, "I've hardly heard any news from the big city since I moved here. Anything exciting going on?"

It took Laurel only a second to rally, and then she filled Maureen in on all the latest local New York news.

"When I left, there was a big story in and out of the news," Maureen said, choosing her words carefully. "Had to do with a murderer and the female cop who sent him up."

Laurel nodded, all hint of tears gone, though her voice was still a bit shaky. "The cop's name was Maureen Maguire."

"That's probably why I remember the story," Maureen said. "We have the same first name." *Steady now.*

"She was an amazing woman, really," Laurel said, leaning back against the end of the bed, her sandaled feet out in front of her. "As young as she was, she was already a full detective with the NYPD. I admired her a lot."

Maureen rarely cried, and usually only in frustration, which was why the sudden moisture gathering in her eyes felt so odd.

This beautiful reporter was talking about *her.* As a cop, Maureen had gone about her business because she'd had to, because she'd had something she needed to do. She'd never thought anyone else noticed.

"I remember her testimony put the guy in jail for life."

"Carl Nevil," Laurel answered. "She and her partner not only testified against the guy—they were responsible for turning up the evidence and making the arrest. And she talked her informant into coming forward."

"Hard to believe that trial was over a year ago."

"And it's not over yet."

Maureen tensed. "What do you mean?"

"When Nevil was sentenced, he swore that the cops and the informant would be 'taken care of.'" Laurel's voice dropped to mimic the bastard.

"But surely no one took him seriously," Maureen said. "I mean, that kind of thing happens in the movies and on television, not in real life."

Shrugging, Laurel kicked off her sandals and settled herself on the bed, sitting cross-legged. "It happens in real life, too, though I don't know how seriously everyone took him. What I do know is that Nevil had a brother, Owen, who was serving time for conspiracy to murder and was up for parole shortly after Carl's trial. A week after Owen gets out, the informant suddenly gets hit by a car in front of his house. NYPD picked Owen up for questioning, but they had no evidence to prove anything and had to let him go."

"So maybe he didn't do it."

"Seems pretty coincidental, don't you think?"

Yeah. Way too coincidental. "I don't know." Maureen shrugged, though she watched the reporter carefully. "Still sounds like a made-for-TV movie to me. Did anything happen to the woman and her partner?" If Laurel was hiding something, Maureen was going to find out right now.

"The partner retired to Florida. So far as I know, he's busy playing golf with his wife."

"And the female detective?"

"She disappeared. No one knows where she went." There were none of the usual signs that the woman was lying. No raising of the eyes, no fidgeting. "If you want my honest opinion," Laurel said, "I think they put her in the witness protection program."

There hadn't been enough of a threat to warrant that—just enough to possibly get her run over by a car.

"Has anyone tried to find her?"

"Not that I know of," Laurel answered. "Most of my colleagues would sooner hide her away themselves than expose her. It's not too often you come across a cop as dedicated and gifted as she was. Especially in New York City. We seem to more readily breed the jaded type."

Frank Quigg, Maureen's superior, had definitely been jaded. Yet when Maureen told him of her decision to quit the force and move home to Cooper's Corner, he'd not only understood, but fully supported the decision.

That fact had probably scared her most of all.

She wasn't worried so much for herself but for the babies who depended on her. They were already growing up without a father since her ex-husband had left her; she wasn't going to have them motherless, as well.

Not if she could help it.

ALL OF THE GUESTS at Twin Oaks were attending Cooper's Corner's Founders Day barbecue the next day. Though she would have preferred to drive herself so she could change her mind about going at the last minute, Laurel allowed herself to be talked into traveling with most of the other guests—Tom, a single dad with eight- and ten-year-old daughters, and Walter and Doris, an English professor and his homemaker wife.

She was glad to have made that choice when they arrived at the mowed field just outside of town that was the site of the event. White tables and chairs, colorful booths, barbecue grills, tents with tables full of food, games, balloons, a bandstand and crowds of people filled the entire area. With all of those families and friends milling around, people who'd known one another their whole lives, she'd have felt terrible arriving alone.

She'd thought she was ready to come back to Cooper's Corner. To face people that had been part of her other life, people she'd known, loved and left behind. She wasn't so sure anymore.

Walter and Doris split off from their small party as soon as Doris saw the booths selling homemade Cooper's Corner handicrafts. That left Laurel with Tom and his daughters, Sharon and Nancy. She supposed to onlookers they appeared as a family—mom, dad and the kids. And while the idea made her uncomfortable, it also offered an anonymity that she welcomed.

She wasn't ready for the memories.

"Can we do the pony rides, Dad?" Sharon, the oldest of Tom's daughters, asked.

"Fine with me," Tom said, and then looked at Laurel. "You want to come along?"

The light in his eyes and his easy smile offered her a welcome she couldn't resist. "Sure," she said, knowing the relief she felt as she dropped into step beside them didn't bode well for the purpose of her visit to Cooper's Corner—finding a way to be at peace with her past.

With short dark hair and the build of a baseball player, Tom was a handsome man. Not that Laurel was looking, she thought with characteristic apathy. Not with Shane waiting for her back in New York. Shane had told her recently that he loved her. Laurel had wanted to tell him the same, but she couldn't. Not yet.

It was one of the things she struggled with—her inability to let any man take Paul's place in her life.

"Do you know many of these people?" Tom asked as the girls ran ahead to get in line for the pony rides.

"Some," she said, careful to avoid eye contact with the crowds of people. Her heart softened as her gaze landed on an older couple manning the lemonade stand. "That's Dr. Dorn and his wife, Martha," she said, pointing. "He was born here but left to go to medical school. He and Martha returned fifty years later after Felix retired."

"How old are they?" Tom asked.

"In their eighties." Laurel looked away quickly when Martha glanced their way. Chances were she wouldn't be recognized, but just in case… "They weren't here when I lived in town," she added. "I've actually only met them a couple of times on visits, but Felix is an amazing man— always ready to help out. Looks like that's still the case."

There were a lot of people she didn't know, and some she recognized but couldn't place.

The girls rode the ponies, had their faces painted and climbed a portable rock wall that had been brought in for the celebration. A local band filled the air with pop tunes, and when they took a break, Laurel and her small clan joined a crowd watching a play depicting Theodore Cooper's arrival in this remote part of the Massachusetts Berkshires back in the early 1800s.

Laurel and Tom and the girls clapped as enthusiastically as the rest of the townspeople at the play's end, moved by the struggles the early settlers had to endure. It was thanks to their fortitude that the thriving village now stood where once there was only uncleared land. And then the four of them filled paper plates and sat down at a table on the outskirts of the field to eat and watch the towns-people celebrate their heritage.

"This chicken is great," Tom said, licking barbecue sauce from his fingers. The girls had the sauce smeared on their faces and hands.

"I'm sure it came from Ed Taylor," Laurel said, remembering the man with fondness. He had to be close to sixty by now. "He's that skinny man over there at the grill." She licked her fingers, trying not to remember that last time she'd had Ed's chicken. It had been the Fourth of July before Paul's death....

"Ed raises only natural, free-range chickens. Everyone in the village buys from him. His farm neighbors Twin Oaks, but I've heard he has neither electricity nor running water..."

"How does he get drinks?" eight-year-old Nancy asked, wide-eyed.

"He hand-pumps his water from a well," Laurel told the little girl.

There ensued a discussion on the luxuries of modern technology that took them through the end of dinner, into dessert, and continued to pop up throughout the fireworks and the drive back to Twin Oaks, as well. Both of Tom's girls were in awe of old Ed.

Truth be known, Laurel was a bit in awe of him herself. Despite hard times, the man seemed to have a solid grasp on what he wanted out of life, to know what mattered most to him, and the strength to pursue his goals. As she lay in bed that night, listening to the night sounds outside her window, Laurel wished she had half of Ed's peace. She loved her job, but she could have no personal life as long as she clung to the past.

And yet, all night long, instead of confronting her past, she'd purposely avoided speaking to anyone she knew.

Maybe she just wasn't ready.

CHAPTER TWO

MASSACHUSETTS STATE TROOPER Scott Hunter was just toasting a bagel for breakfast when the phone rang. He'd worked late the night before with all the heavy weekend traffic and was having a slow start this morning.

"Scott Hunter." He answered the ring, a cup of coffee poised at his lips. If he got through this day, then he could quit pushing for a while. His two-week vacation, the first full vacation he'd taken in three and a half years, started tomorrow.

The adrenaline that had been absent that morning surged when Scott recognized his captain's voice on the line.

There was a report of a missing person at the new bed-and-breakfast that had opened in Cooper's Corner a couple of days before. Although the police didn't under ordinary circumstances get involved with missing adults since they usually had gone of their own free will, Maureen Cooper, the B and B's co-owner, had requested the favor of a visit from Scott.

Grabbing his bagel, Scott buckled on his holster over his work blues and was out the door.

THOUGH HE'D LIVED IN Cooper's Corner most of his life, Scott had not yet been inside Twin Oaks Bed & Breakfast. He'd driven by it many times when it was still a private residence owned by bachelor Warren Cooper, and later, while the remodeling was going on.

The Cooper family history was legend around these parts, and Warren had added his own chapter.

Though he'd never married, Warren had a shocking secret in his past. A brief affair with the woman he had loved his entire life had resulted in the birth of twin girls, but Warren and his lover, Helen Webb, could never acknowledge he was the babies' father. They had turned to each other when news came that Helen's husband had been killed in the war—news that had later proved to be a mistake.

Helen bore Warren's children as her husband's. One of the babies had died as an infant in her crib, and the other grew up to have three children of her own before she died, too, never knowing that Warren was her father.

Only on his deathbed, a few months after Helen's death, did Warren confess his secret. All three of his grandchildren were notified, and they'd all come to visit in Cooper's Corner that past year.

Yes, Scott knew the history of Twin Oaks, he thought as he drove up the tree-lined drive. Warren had left the family homestead to his brother's children, Clint and Maureen, and Scott was only sorry his first visit had to do with work.

The minute he stepped inside the front door, Maureen and Clint both started talking about William Byrd, describing a sophisticated older gentleman who had seemed to be enjoying his stay.

"Byrd didn't show up for breakfast this morning," Clint was saying.

"Which was a bit odd," Maureen explained, "since he enjoyed Clint's walnut griddle cakes so much yesterday and mentioned that he was looking forward to having them again.''

"But it wasn't until he didn't show up for checkout time that we knew he was missing," her brother continued.

"Have you checked Byrd's room?" Scott asked, frowning.

"Only to make certain that he wasn't there," Maureen said, her lips pinched. "The lock was stuck so we had to use a crowbar to pull the door away from the jamb."

Scott stiffened. "It had been tampered with?"

"No." The pair shook their heads as Maureen explained. "It's been sticking. We just didn't know it had gotten that bad. It was scheduled for maintenance tomorrow."

"What about a car? I'm assuming he drove himself here."

Clint nodded. "A rental," he said. "Black BMW. It's not here."

Could mean that the man left of his own free will and met up with trouble somewhere else. Somewhere completely unrelated to Twin Oaks. Or maybe he wasn't in trouble at all.

He could also just have partied a little too hard the night before and hadn't made it home yet. Though that didn't sound like the fastidious older man the Coopers had described.

"When was the last time Byrd was seen?"

"Breakfast yesterday morning," Maureen and Clint said in unison.

Brother and sister stood together in the gathering room at Twin Oaks, forming a solid wall against whatever came their way. A pain, sharp and unsuspecting, knifed through

Scott as he witnessed their solidarity, followed by a longing he couldn't deny.

And a guilt that ate insidiously at his insides. A guilt he couldn't escape.

But he could push it away. He'd become quite adept at pushing it away. After all, he'd had three and a half years of practice. And a job that was all consuming when he let it be.

A job he was going to do. Now.

"Who else is here?" he asked, his full concentration back on the case.

All but one of the guests had checked out, and Clint's son, Keegan, was watching Maureen's children in the kitchen.

"Laurel, our fourth guest, decided to stay on for a couple more days," Maureen confided. "She's upstairs, I believe."

Scott looked down at the notepad he'd pulled from his pocket and jotted aimlessly.

Laurel. A name he hadn't heard in a long time. And one with which he tortured himself far too often.

For a fleeting second he wondered what "his" Laurel was doing at that moment. Working on some big news story, no doubt. Last he'd heard she'd become a hotshot reporter in New York.

And he was a hotshot detective with the Massachusetts state police. He looked up from the pad, away from the name he'd scrawled.

"Did anyone notice anything suspicious about Byrd at breakfast yesterday?" he asked.

"To the contrary." Clint shook his head. "He was in a good mood and enjoyed talking to the other guests. In fact," he added, "we'd been feeling very hopeful since he seemed so pleased with everything. A good review from him would pretty much guarantee our success.''

Having the travel writer mysteriously disappear from Twin Oaks on their opening weekend was going to do exactly the opposite, Scott reckoned.

Determined to get to the bottom of the man's disappearance as quickly as possible, he asked, ''Do either of you have any reason to suspect that someone might be out to sabotage your efforts here?''

Clint and Maureen exchanged a long glance, then Clint shrugged. Maureen turned to Scott.

''Clint doesn't think so.'' She glanced at her brother apologetically. ''It's just…''

''Just?''

She sighed. ''Until almost a year ago, I was a detective with the New York Police Department.''

Scott whistled. The Cooper's Corner grapevine had missed that one. But then—considering Warren's amazing story—secrets weren't uncommon with the Cooper clan.

''You retired awfully young,'' Scott said.

Maureen shrugged, her long brown hair falling around her shoulders. ''Yeah, well, it wasn't quite the way I'd envisioned,'' she said, her New York accent more evident now. After being assured what she was telling him would go no further, she told him about Carl Nevil, the murderer she'd put away well over a year ago. ''He swore he'd get his revenge,'' she said, her voice steady, though Scott saw her barely perceptible shiver.

''That's not all that uncommon,'' Scott said. ''Empty threats made in the heat of the moment.''

Maureen shook her head. ''Carl's brother, Owen, was in prison at the time of Carl's conviction, doing time for conspiracy to commit murder. He's been up on drug charges, too, but is out on parole now. A week after Owen was released, the man I'd talked into turning state's evidence for Carl's case was killed by a hit-and-run driver outside his own apartment.

"That's when I determined that I had to get out of New York for good," Maureen explained. "If it were just me, I'd have stayed and gotten the bastard, but I had the twins to think about. I couldn't take a chance on leaving them motherless, or worse, on Owen Nevil using them to get at me."

"The twins are what, three?" Scott asked, still writing in his book. He had a razor-sharp mind and rarely referred to the notes he took while working on a case. But he took them, anyway, for form's sake.

"Just."

He nodded.

"My records at the department have been sealed and I'm using my maiden name—on the force I was known by my married name, Maguire."

Scott's brows rose. "You're still married?"

"Divorced."

"How long?"

"A little over three years."

"Right after your daughters were born?" By the sounds of things, this woman had not had an easy life.

"Before," she said. "I was two months pregnant when Chance, my ex-husband, walked out."

Great guy.

"Have you considered the fact that Owen Nevil might have arranged to have Byrd disappear as some kind of warning, telling you that while you'd run from the city, changed your name and had your records sealed, you've still been found?"

"Yes." The former NYPD detective spoke volumes with the single word.

Clint nodded as well, his chestnut hair—a shade darker than his sister's—falling over his forehead. "We talked about the possibility, but it's not likely, is it?"

Shrugging, Scott said, "I sure don't think so. There's no telling what the criminal mind will find satisfying, but at this point, we'll assume your secret is still safe from the Nevils."

Still, just because he liked all of his bases covered, Scott asked Maureen for contact information for Frank Quigg, her old boss in New York. He'd follow up on the hoodlum and his convict brother as soon as he finished at Twin Oaks.

"Shall we go up and take a look at the room?" he asked.

"I'd rather stay down here if you don't mind," Maureen surprised him by saying.

"I'll take you up," Clint added, pulling a big brass key from the pocket of his slacks.

With a raised brow, Scott glanced at Maureen. The woman was as qualified as he was to do this job—maybe more so.

"Chances are this whole thing has nothing to do with the Nevils, and I don't want to do anything to tip anyone off about my previous life," she explained without his asking. "My suddenly exhibiting detective skills could certainly start people wondering—and talking."

She made good sense, though Scott didn't think he could have made the same decision. He'd have needed to take control. "Could you see if you can find the one guest you said was still here? I'd like to question her as soon as Clint and I finish upstairs," he asked before turning to follow her brother.

Maureen nodded. Her livelihood—perhaps her life itself—was on the line and she appeared amazingly composed.

Scott had a feeling NYPD had lost one hell of a detective when she'd retired.

BYRD'S ROOM WAS AT THE FAR end of the corridor. Though there were some personal effects lying around, the room had a deserted air. The colorful handmade quilt spread neatly across the top of the pine four-poster bed was evidence of the fact that the bed had not been slept in. The plate of cookies on the nightstand hadn't been touched.

"When were those left there?" Scott asked.

"Yesterday afternoon."

Also on the nightstand, next to the cookies, was a copy of Byrd's bestselling book on bed-and-breakfasts, an old photo of a young couple in an amorous embrace used as a bookmark.

Scott took note of everything—both mentally and on paper—touching as little as possible. There was an overnight duffel on the floor by the nightstand. A silk nightgown hung from one of the bedposts and on the dresser was a laptop and a thirty-five-year-old birth certificate for someone called Leslie Renwick. The birth had taken place in Iowa, and the parents' names were whited out.

"Look at this," Scott said.

Clint, who'd been standing in the doorway, crossed over and glanced down at the birth certificate.

"Who would just throw an important document like this on the top of a dresser?" he asked.

"Someone who wasn't intending to leave it there."

"Someone who left here in a hurry, you mean?" Clint asked, frowning as he gave Scott a sideways glance.

"Possibly." Scott looked back at the dresser. While

there was no real indication that William Byrd had been kidnapped, he was getting a bad feeling about the whole thing. "You know anyone named Leslie Renwick?" he asked Clint.

Clint shook his head. "Never heard of her."

"She's not from around here," Scott said. He'd lived in Cooper's Corner most of his life and was only a year younger than Ms. Renwick. If she lived around here, he'd know her. "As a matter of fact, I don't know any Renwicks in the area."

"I don't, either," Clint said. "Not now and not from back when I lived here as a kid, either."

"You were, what, nine, when your family moved to New York?" Scott asked. He didn't know much about Clint, except that he was a former architect-turned-innkeeper, a widower with a twelve-year-old son.

Clint nodded, turning slowly and studying the room. "I wonder if the name means anything to Maureen."

"Good question." Scott took another look around as well. "We'll ask her as soon as we get downstairs."

"You looked in the duffel?" Clint asked.

"Yeah, nothing there but a change of clothes and the usual toiletries."

Clint shook his head. "Wouldn't you think he'd have taken them if he was planning to be gone overnight?"

Avoiding the other man's eyes, Scott said, "Just because he didn't plan to be gone doesn't mean that it wasn't his choice not to return."

He made a couple more notes on his pad and then slid it into the front pocket of his blue uniform shirt. "We can head back down for now," he told Clint. "Mind if I keep the key to this room?"

It had opened without the use of a crowbar this time.

"Of course not." Clint hesitated at the door. "Tell me,

Officer, how much of a chance do you think there is that Nevil's behind this somehow?''

''Ten, maybe twenty percent.''

Scott tried to ignore the pang of compassion he felt as the other man's gaze reflected his worry.

Scott had a job to do. That's all that mattered. Ever.

Maureen met them at the bottom of the stairs, her jade-green eyes filled with questions—and frustration. She was probably chafing to get in on the investigation herself, Scott realized.

Like Clint, she had never heard of a Leslie Renwick, either.

''Laurel's waiting for you in the gathering room,'' she told Scott as Clint excused himself to check on the kids in the kitchen. ''If you don't mind, I think I'll head back to my office and see if I can reach the other two families that were here, though I doubt they've had time to get home yet.''

Scott nodded, forcing himself not to think back to the Laurel who had once been part of his life.

Shoulders straight, he headed purposefully off to the gathering room to complete the interrogation. He was eager to get to his phone and call in some favors. Put an unofficial trace on Byrd's missing rental car and on Owen Nevil. He also wanted to go back upstairs and see what he could do with that computer.

He was hoping it would yield some clues.

SHE WAS STARING OUT the window. Scott stood in the opening to the gigantic living room at Twin Oaks and sucked in air.

Heart pounding, he couldn't move. Just stared.

She had her back to him, but that didn't matter. He knew her silhouette front, back and sideways. Recognized the way she held her shoulders completely straight, her neck stiff. That meant she was trying to figure something out—or to remember something.

But even if he hadn't paid undue attention to things that weren't his business, he'd still have known it was her. No one else had that yellow hair, though it was shoulder length now.

She was dressed casually in navy capris, a white blouse and white leather sandals. The outfit might have appeared ordinary on someone else, but on Laurel it was pure elegance.

Laurel. Here. Close again.

CHAPTER THREE

SCOTT WAS STUNNED.

He'd dreamed Laurel London into Cooper's Corner a million times, even as he'd fully accepted that he was never going to see her again. He could hardly believe it. The excruciating pleasure—and agony—that she instilled within his most private self lunged at him mercilessly.

He opened his mouth to speak—to call out to her—and had nothing to say.

How did a man calmly say hello to a woman whose heart he'd broken? Whose dreams he'd shattered with the horrible news he'd given her. How did he call out to her, remembering that she'd made it clear she wanted nothing to do with him, that seeing him was too painful to her?

Thoughts flitted so rapidly across the page of Scott's mental notebook, he could hardly keep up with them. Standing there close to Laurel brought the pain of Paul's passing forcefully to the surface.

After three and a half years of mourning his older brother, he'd become pretty adept at keeping that ache locked away.

Right along with the shame of having been so desperately in love with Laurel himself. This woman had been his brother's fiancée—left at the altar when Paul's life had been cruelly snatched away the morning of their wedding.

Images of his brother's mangled body, thrown from the car when his seat belt ripped from its casing, flashed across the mental page. He'd known Paul was dead the moment he climbed from the wreckage and stumbled over to the grassy embankment where his brother's body had landed. Paul's head had been bent at such an unnatural angle. And the blood trickling out of his mouth and down his chin would have choked him had he been breathing....

Scott hadn't even had a scratch that bled. Not one goddamned scratch. Yet he was the one who should have been lying in a heap with a broken neck.

The sedan they'd been in that morning had been Scott's. He was supposed to have been driving his brother from Boston, where Paul had his new law practice, back home to Cooper's Corner for Paul's wedding. He was the one trained to deal with the icy weather conditions.

And he would have been the one in the driver's seat, wearing the seat belt that had broken when they hit the patch of ice and flipped, but he'd been so damned hungover he'd practically seen double.

He'd put away so much eighty proof the night before at Paul's bachelor party that they could have sterilized medical instruments with his blood. And all because of this woman.

He'd drunk himself into a stupor to forget the fact that the following day his beloved older brother was marrying the only woman Scott was ever going to love.

Laurel turned and found him staring at her.

"Scott?" The word was both a whisper and a cry.

He nodded, needing to hold out his arms to her, to crush her to him and promise her that somehow he'd make amends, make things right for her.

But he couldn't.

There were some things a man just couldn't do, no matter how determined he was.

How in hell could he dare to offer solace when he was

the reason she was suffering in the first place? When he hadn't even been man enough to tell her that he was responsible for her fiancé's death?

If she'd read any of the reports, she'd know Paul had been driving that morning, but she'd been in such shock, run out so immediately, chances were she'd never seen a write-up of the accident. And even if she had, the underlying facts, the heavy ones that Scott's conscience carried around every single day, the ones that crucified him were nothing that would show up in a report.

Only Scott's father had known those. And now he, too, was gone.

She ran over and threw her arms around his neck, embracing him completely. Silently, he wrapped his arms around her, holding her to him as he fought back the needy shudder that passed through him.

In the next second she was crying, sobs racking her body. Tears burned the back of his eyes as they shared a pain too deep to put into any kind of words. No matter what else had come between them, what wrongs he'd been guilty of, they'd both loved Paul fiercely.

Scott's older brother had been the kind of man who instilled such love in those he cared about. And loyalty, too... For both of them, the loss of Paul meant that life would never be the same again.

After long moments consumed by grief, Laurel pulled back from Scott, her dove-gray eyes limpid with tears. Gently, unable to help himself, he pushed the strands of tear-dampened hair away from her cheeks.

"I'm sorry," she said almost awkwardly, her arms falling to her sides as she put more distance between them. "I guess this weekend's been harder than I thought."

"You've been in town all weekend?"

He didn't know why that thought was just striking him

now. Or why the fact that she hadn't contacted him was so painful.

She'd had no reason to contact him. And every reason not to.

"I came to say goodbye," she said softly. "I need to get on with my life."

The words struck a chord of irrational fear in Scott's chest, as though Laurel had found a peace he'd been denied.

He couldn't say goodbye. He had no life to get on with. There was just existence left. And work.

He didn't deserve anything else.

She'd never given him a hint of encouragement, yet he'd allowed his love for her to cloud everything around him and lead him to a foolishness that had cost his brother his life. Yet even as he'd been telling Laurel the terrible news about Paul's death just hours after it had happened, he'd been in love with her. He'd wanted to run away with her, lose himself—his grief—in her arms.

And now, more than three years and a whole load of guilt later, he had a very strong suspicion that he loved her still.

LAUREL COULDN'T STOP TREMBLING.

Coming back to Cooper's Corner had been like rubbing salt in wounds not quite healed enough to withstand the onslaught. Seeing Scott ripped those wounds wide open again, as though in three and a half years there'd been not one fraction of healing.

He looked incredibly good, so tall and strong and solid. Seeing him in his dark blue uniform, one could be tricked into believing that he could really right wrongs. Save the needy. Make the world a better place.

His dark hair was exactly as she remembered, and those striking blue eyes...

"I thought I was ready," she said, when a fresh spate of tears struck.

"You didn't expect to see me." He stood, hands in his pockets, just inches away.

"I thought you'd moved to Boston. You'd just taken that detective position."

"After...the accident...I applied with the state police instead...."

She and Paul had moved to Boston a few years before the accident, when Paul had been accepted at Harvard law school. She had already graduated from the University of Massachusetts with a degree in journalism and had accepted a position at the *Boston Globe,* working on the local desk.

Scott had been planning to move to Boston right after the wedding, keeping the Hunter home in Cooper's Corner as a vacation place. He'd wanted to be closer to their ailing father, who was in an assisted living facility in Boston, but his father had died shortly after the accident. Laurel knew that. She'd sent a card....

After the accident she'd run away from Boston almost as quickly as she'd vacated Cooper's Corner.

"So...you've been here...all these years?"

"Yes."

She was warmed by the way he was looking at her.

"I moved to New York," she told him.

"I know. I've seen you on the news a time or two when I've been on the road."

She was glad. Though when Scott's presence had become a comfort to her rather than the sharp pain it had been the last time she'd seen him, she didn't know.

Maybe she *had* healed some.

"They say time heals all pain, but I don't think the ache is ever going to go away." Private by nature, she'd never have said such a thing to anyone else, but she sensed that Scott would understand. She had a feeling he knew exactly what she meant.

He nodded.

"He should be here," she said.

"I know."

She should be living in Cooper's Corner. Raising Paul's babies. They'd had it all planned.

"I never intended to be a career woman," Laurel confessed.

"From what I've seen, you're very good at what you do. A natural."

She shrugged, unusually pleased by his praise. "I love the work, the challenge, the fact that there's always something new...."

"Keeps your mind busy..."

"So you don't have too much time to think."

They nodded as they recognized in each other some of the suffering they'd thought they bore alone.

And then it was too much for Laurel. She couldn't go back to the places Scott was taking her. Couldn't cry enough tears to ease the grief.

Being shuffled from foster home to foster home most of her life, Laurel had never had a real family to call her own, never belonged anywhere, never knew what home felt like, until she'd met Paul. She'd been eagerly accepted into the all-male Hunter clan. There'd only been the three of them, Paul, Scott and their father, but they'd been all Laurel had ever dreamed of in a family.

She didn't dream anymore.

"Speaking of jobs," she said, distancing herself physically as she broke the emotional connection between her and Scott, "Maureen said you're here about Mr. Byrd's disappearance." She crossed over to the piano that dominated one corner of the room.

His head tilted slightly as he appeared to adjust to the changed atmosphere between them. "Yeah," he said, straightening as he drew a small notebook from his shirt pocket and came farther into the room. "I don't know how much time you have, so I'll be as quick as I can."

"I have all the time you need." She leaned an elbow against the piano, trying to convince herself that she was relaxed. Trying not to admit to herself how badly she needed that piece of solid furniture to hold her up. "As a matter of fact, I was hoping to be able to help." She attempted an easy grin. "After all, investigation is a big part of what I do."

At first she was afraid he was going to refuse.

"I'm not ready to leave Cooper's Corner," she confessed. "I don't feel like I've finished doing what I came here to do.

"Officially I'm on vacation, but I need something to do. I've even got my tape recorder upstairs." She tried for a chuckle that ended up a weak smile. "I never go anywhere without it. This could prove to be a great human interest story and I'd have the exclusive."

Of course, she only covered local stuff, but…

Scott was frowning down at his notebook.

She took his silence as a sign that he wasn't completely averse to the idea—maybe he just needed to be convinced. "You know, the benefits of 'keeping your mind busy.'"

"Three and a half years ago you could hardly bear to be in my presence."

"I know."

"The police aren't going to be officially involved— they can't be. There's been no crime committed."

"I know."

His gaze met and held hers for a long time.

Laurel braced herself for any one of the myriad questions she sensed were buzzing inside his mind. Scott never had been one to hide things. To the contrary. His need to have everything out on the table had been disconcerting at times. Scott Hunter had no time for subtlety.

To someone as private as Laurel, Scott's openness had been incredibly unnerving, and yet comforting as well. She'd known right from the beginning, and never had cause to doubt from that time on, that she held a very important place in the Hunter family.

Only Paul had known how much she'd coveted that position.

"Okay."

"What?" Though she didn't move from her position at the piano, Laurel's heart rate sped up.

"I said okay. We'll do this one together. But if it gets dangerous, you do as I say."

"Of course."

"Then as of now, we're a team."

And suddenly, as much as she'd been seeking just that response, Laurel had doubts.

She truly wanted to do whatever she could to help find William Byrd. And though she didn't really understand why, she felt compelled to spend this time with Scott, too.

Was it to finally put the past to rest?

Or because she couldn't let go?

It was the confusion of seeing Scott again that made her unsure, and a little afraid, of this temporary commitment.

"So…" Scott took a seat at the thick oak game table on one side of the room, pushing out a chair for Laurel with his foot. "Let's get started with you telling me what you know. I'll fill you in and then we'll go take a look at Byrd's room again.''

Appreciating his professional air, Laurel pushed away from the piano and moved over to join Scott, more comfortable with herself as she slipped into a professional role herself.

She told him what she knew, which wasn't much. She hadn't seen Byrd since breakfast the morning before.

"I asked the others before they left this morning if they'd seen him, but no one had," she told him.

"You've already questioned the other guests?"

Laurel nodded. "I wondered why he wasn't at breakfast, and I guess it's just habit to ask questions when something's afoot.''

"This is great." Scott jotted something in his notebook. "What else did they say?"

"Not a whole lot." There were no real clues as far as Laurel could tell. "We all went to the barbecue in town yesterday. No one remembered seeing William there."

"There's been no report of any accidents in the area, and Clint said he'd checked the local hospitals just in case.''

"Something unexpected had to have happened." Laurel said aloud what she'd been thinking all morning. "He was perfectly relaxed at breakfast yesterday—a weekend vacationer like the rest of us. William had a great sense of humor, dry, witty. He kept us all laughing. He was like everyone's favorite uncle." She paused, thinking about the still-commanding figure of the older man. Though mostly bald, he'd been in great shape, muscular and trim. "I know he was planning to attend the barbecue," she continued, "because he told me he'd see me there...."

While Scott scribbled in his notebook, Laurel itched to get to her tape recorder. And then it dawned on her that this situation was far different from the stuff she normally did. Usually the subject of a story agreed to interviews before she ever began. She probably wasn't going to be able to have her recorder on during an unofficial police investigation.

"Seems kind of silly for us both to be taking notes as we do this," she said aloud, remembering what a meticulous note-taker Scott was in school. Notes that she'd borrowed, along with most of his friends. Though never, as far as she knew, did he use them himself. "Do you mind, if I do end up doing a story, if I borrow your notes?"

"Not at all."

"Thanks." She smiled at him, and he smiled back. And nothing made sense for a second.

"So," Scott said, maybe a little more loudly than necessary, "did Byrd give any sign of being preoccupied? Was he wearing wrinkled or mismatched clothes, losing track of the conversation, lapsing off into silence?"

Shaking her head, Laurel clasped her hands and rested them on top of the table. "Nope. He was meticulous. In his dress and in his manners."

Scott glanced up from his notebook, catching her off guard. The instant intensity that flared between them shook her. Badly.

"Shall we go up and take a look?"

Laurel nodded, almost pathetic in her relief as he broke the spell. Dazed, she followed Scott upstairs to William Byrd's room.

"We're going to find William," she told Scott, forcing her mind to concentrate on the only thing that mattered. "And he's going to be just fine."

And because she was so sure of that, she felt a bit uncomfortable as Scott worked the key in the sticky lock until he got it to open. She felt she was invading William's privacy. But she was also very eager to get inside and see what she could find out about his disappearance.

Somehow William's safe return had linked itself in Laurel's mind to her own ability to move on with her life. As though in order for her trip back to Cooper's Corner to be successful on one level, it had to be successful on all levels. If she couldn't help William, she couldn't hope to help herself. It was illogical, but very real just the same.

"I did a surface scan when I was up here earlier," Scott told her as they entered the room. "This time I want to know about the dust particles in the corners."

They looked under the bed, in the drawers, behind every piece of furniture.

Laurel crossed to the dresser, using a pencil to type on the laptop keyboard.

"This computer's password-encrypted," she told Scott.

He joined her by the dresser, looking over her shoulder at the darkened screen. "Must be something important in there…"

"Something that could, perhaps, put William in danger…."

"Except why would he have left it sitting here like this?"

"For that matter, why would he have left it out in the open like this at all…"

"…unless he didn't plan to be away from it," Scott concluded.

Laurel felt a rush of familiar warmth as her mind melded with Scott's. The two of them had always thought more alike than she and Paul had.

Paul had teased them about it.

And she'd punished him with heated kisses…

"But then, writers are by nature a somewhat paranoid bunch," she said, refusing to allow herself to be sidetracked. "It's probably more likely that William is simply protecting his next bestseller."

"What do you make of this?" With the back of his hand, Scott nudged the birth certificate until it was facing them and more clearly legible.

Laurel whistled softly. "The birth was thirty-five years ago. In Iowa. And..."

"No parents."

"I wonder who Leslie Renwick is...."

"I've never heard of any Renwick family around here. Maureen and Clint hadn't, either."

"It's got to be significant, though. People don't just leave important documents like that lying around."

Scott pulled a cell phone out of his pocket and dialed some numbers.

While he gave the specifics of the birth certificate to whoever was on the other end of the line, Laurel moved on to look at the copy of Byrd's B and B guide on the nightstand.

"It's open to a place in Vermont," she said as soon as Scott hung up the phone. "I wonder if that means anything."

Again, Scott came to stand closely beside her. Again, Laurel reacted strangely, feeling an odd combination of security and excitement. Scott was reminding her of Paul—reigniting the torch that had burned so brightly for her fiancé.

Was she ever going to be over her intense love for Paul? Had she set herself an impossible goal in believing she could move on?

"Might be someplace he was planning to visit. I'll give them a call, see what I can find out," Scott was saying as he jotted down the phone number and address. "What do you make of the picture?"

Laurel glanced at the old photograph, briefly. A young couple hugging was not what she needed to be focusing on right now. Turning from the nightstand, she noticed the negligee hanging on the bedpost.

"I wonder if the picture has any connection to that," she said, pointing to the sexy nightgown.

"Perhaps," Scott said, inspecting the gown as closely as he could without actually touching it. "I'm guessing that what it does mean is that a woman plays a significant part in whatever happened to Byrd yesterday."

"Unless he was a cross-dresser..."

CHAPTER FOUR

AFTER PULLING A FEW STRINGS to have Byrd's possessions sent down to the lab in Pittsfield for fingerprinting, Scott invited Laurel to take a drive into Cooper's Corner with him to do some questioning. Depending on what he turned up, Scott figured he just might be spending the better part of his vacation working on the case.

Chances were someone had seen William Byrd the day before, or at least seen the unfamiliar BMW driving through town. Cooper's Corner wasn't that big. A nice car like Byrd's rental was bound to have been noticed.

Focusing on business took Scott as far as the end of Twin Oaks's drive. He'd filed all of the current clues in his mind and was in a holding pattern until he had something more to assimilate. As it was, speculation could lead him in very different directions and he didn't want to be heading the wrong way when the right clue came in. That was how detectives *didn't* solve cases.

But without the diversion of the case, he had only Laurel to think about. Just having her in the Blazer with him, inhaling that hint of lilacs, created an ache he'd spent the past three and a half years trying to avoid.

"It's great to see you again." The words broke free of the restraints he'd put on them, but Scott wasn't surprised. He was the most self-controlled person he knew—until he was with Laurel London.

It had always been that way, and he hated it. Hated

himself for it. He'd spent many fruitless hours trying to figure out why one person, and one person only, in the entire universe could do this to him.

She glanced over at him and smiled. "It's good to see you, too."

"Don't sound so surprised."

"Oh, it's nothing against you, Scott, it's just..."

"I know."

Sitting there next to him, she had to be aching far more than he was. While the woman he loved was right beside him, still bringing him a measure of exquisite pleasure, the man she loved was dead, gone from her forever.

Because of him.

He'd bet his life she wouldn't be finding it good to see him again if she knew that.

"Remember that exposé you did about the foster-care system back in high school?" he asked. It seemed prudent to remind himself of the not-so-warm feelings she'd had for him at one time.

"You mean the one you found in my notebook and submitted to the school newspaper without my permission?" she asked, her voice filled with the feistiness that only those closest to her ever witnessed.

"It was damn good," he said. "Too good to go the way of everything else you wrote." He jumped right into his side of the familiar argument, feeling more in control by the second.

It was an argument that had never been resolved. And if history was at all reliable, it could easily occupy the few minutes it was going to take to get them to Cooper's General Store.

"It was highly personal, not meant to be seen by anyone but Paul."

"It's not my fault he left it out. My dad read it, too."

"But he didn't steal it."

"I didn't steal it," Scott said defensively. "I borrowed it. Your insights were too intensely on the mark to be wasted. People needed to hear what you had to say, not only for your sake, but for all of the other kids who were being shuffled around like you'd been."

"And that was reason enough to plaster my innermost feelings all over the state without even so much as asking me first?"

"I didn't plaster them all over the state. I had nothing to do with that," Scott said, relaxing as the old adrenaline pumped through him. Town was right head. He could see the weathered bronze statue of the Revolutionary War soldier standing guard in the village green, his rifle and bayonet held proudly upright. "I can't help the fact that Warren Cooper picked up the article."

"Or that someone sent it to the *Boston Globe,* too?"

"It wasn't me," he told her for the hundredth time.

"I don't believe you."

"And I don't know how to convince you. But I didn't do it."

"Who do you think did?"

His gaze shot over to her. It wasn't a question she'd ever asked before. Did that mean she was actually starting to believe him on this? It had been the only time in their entire eighteen-year history that she hadn't believed him about something. And this wasn't the one time he'd lied to her.

He couldn't let the fact that she was softening mean anything.

Not one damn thing.

"I'm not sure," he admitted, wishing like hell that he knew who'd sent that article to the *Boston Globe.* And how they'd been able to print it without permission from the author.

Because she'd just assumed it was Scott and hadn't wanted to attract more attention to herself, Laurel had never pursued the issue. At least those were the reasons she'd given him. And the reason she hadn't turned him in for forging her permission to use the article in the school paper.

"You still shouldn't have given it to the school paper without my permission."

"I know."

"Wow!" Scott's groin tightened at the laughingly condescending tone in her voice. "Miracles do happen on occasion," she said. "I never thought you'd admit that you were wrong on this one."

He wasn't sure why he had.

"But since you have," Laurel said, her voice dangerously soft. "I need to thank you."

"For admitting I was wrong?"

"No, for submitting it in the first place."

What? He almost swerved into the gravel on the shoulder of the road.

"I owe my entire career to that article," she said, spinning his world into confusion.

"How so?"

"I'm such a private person, I never would have submitted anything to anyone. Yet it was all the reaction I got from that article, from people who told me that it made a difference to them, that showed me what I needed to do with my life. Until that article came out I never knew I had any talent for writing."

"You have an uncanny ability to get the facts, to filter through them without apparent bias, and then present a sometimes new truth about whatever subject you report on.''

''Thank you.''

Her gratitude didn't sit well with him, because he knew how very much he didn't deserve it.

Luckily he'd just pulled into the parking lot and didn't have to reply.

NERVES TAUT, LAUREL WATCHED silently as Scott found a parking spot at Cooper's General Store. Philo and Phyllis Cooper were legends in Cooper's Corner. A distant cousin to Maureen and Clint Cooper, Philo had lived in the village every one of his fifty-seven years, and his fifty-five-year-old wife was a local girl as well.

It wasn't that Laurel disliked the older couple. To the contrary, she'd found them a pure delight when she'd first moved to town and had spent hours hanging around their store, learning all she could about the town she'd decided was going to be her hometown.

No matter what was going on in Cooper's Corner, Philo and Phyllis knew all about it and were only too happy to give every detail to anyone who asked.

''Smart choice, coming here first,'' she said as they got out of the truck.

''Do I detect a note of sarcasm?'' he asked.

''Absolutely not! Why would you say that?''

''Sometimes the Coopers' eagerness to pass on their knowledge is misinterpreted. Some people don't understand that there is nothing malicious about their gossip.''

''Of course there isn't!'' she agreed. ''They share the good just as much as the bad.''

''They're great examples of a small community's belief in the right of everyone to know exactly what's going on in everyone else's life.''

Laurel really liked how adamantly he was defending his town. But he didn't need to defend it to her. Cooper's Corner was her town, too…. Or at least the closest thing she'd ever had to a town she could claim.

"If it hadn't been for Phyllis Cooper," Laurel said, "no one would have known about that time old Mrs. Lathgate broke her hip. The poor woman would have had to cope on her own."

"What about the time Lance Brown had that trouble out at the farm and practically every man in Cooper's Corner ended up out there one weekend, getting a month's worth of work done in two days."

"Wasn't that the time the Browns ended up throwing that huge impromptu barn dance?"

That night was one she'd never forget. It was the first time Paul Hunter had ever spoken to her. She'd been in Cooper's Corner about a year. She was only fifteen years old and he'd been seventeen at the time—a senior. He'd asked her to dance. And she'd never looked at another man since that night. Impossible to believe that was more than eighteen years ago.

"If I'm not mistaken, it was Phyllis Cooper who arranged that dance—and their general store that donated all of the food. A way of saying thank-you for everyone's hard work."

Laurel hadn't known that. Or hadn't remembered. But she wasn't surprised to find it so.

Philo was standing toward the front of the store, talking to an older gentleman Laurel didn't recognize. He looked just as she remembered him. Not tall, stocky, dressed in overalls, with salt-and-pepper hair that never seemed to get more salty.

Laurel had seen him and his wife the night before at the barbecue, but had managed to avoid them. By staying close to the other guests at Twin Oaks, she'd actually avoided recognition by anyone who might have known her.

"Philo, you got a minute?" Scott asked the second the shopkeeper was free.

"Sure, Scott!" Philo said, patting the younger man on the back. "What's up? Nothing official I hope?"

"Well," Scott said, "in a way it is. I was wondering if perhaps you and Phyllis could spare me a couple of minutes for some questions."

Philo's kind eyes darkened. "No one we know's in trouble, are they?"

"I don't think so," Scott said quietly, nodding as a middle-aged man left with a bag full of some kind of hardware.

Philo looked over, seeming to notice Laurel for the first time. She smiled tentatively under his scrutiny. "Pretty young lady you got there, Scott. Someone we should know?"

"You do know her..." Scott was saying, just as Philo blinked, shaking his head.

"Laurel?" he asked. "Is that our Laurel London?"

Laurel grinned, feeling for a second like a prodigal daughter returned home to a loving father.

Except that she'd never had a father, loving or otherwise.

"Laurel London!" Philo exclaimed, his smile widening as he reached his arms out to Laurel.

Not a hugger by nature, she didn't even hesitate as she stepped into that embrace, feeling her throat tighten with emotion.

"How you doing, Philo?" she asked when the older man let her go.

"Can't complain," he said, still grinning at her. "I hear you went to the big city and got yourself a fancy TV job."

"Laurel? Laurel London?" Laurel was saved from Philo's inquisition by an enthusiastic greeting from his wife. A greeting that was only different from his in that it was even more physical in nature. Phyllis not only gave Laurel a long, tight hug, but kissed both of her cheeks as well.

"I've been wondering if you'd ever come back to us," Phyllis said, tears gathering in her eyes.

The motherly woman was a beautiful sight to Laurel.

"I just needed some time," Laurel told her softly. She couldn't lie to Phyllis. She didn't think anyone could keep things from the gentle, giving woman.

Scott shifted beside her, and Philo said, "Scott's here to ask us some questions." Then he looked back at Laurel, a worried frown creasing his brow.

"You aren't in any trouble, are you, my dear?"

"Of course not," Scott said before Laurel could reply. "Laurel's helping me with the investigation."

"It's what she does for television in New York," Phyllis told her husband as though he might actually not have been in possession of that information himself. She led them all back to the office at the rear of the store, instructing Philo to bring in a couple of extra chairs for Laurel and Scott.

The Coopers were distraught when they heard that one of Twin Oaks's guests was missing. But when Scott described William to them, neither could remember seeing him.

"He was driving a black BMW," Laurel said. "A rental. You didn't happen to notice it around town, did you?"

"Yes!" Phyllis cried, sitting forward. "I think I did see it."

"When? Where?" Scott's gaze was intent, his pen poised over the notebook he'd taken from his pocket.

"Saturday afternoon, just down the street."

"You're sure?" Scott asked.

"Positive. I was just on my way from the store back down to the barbecue. I had to come back to get more coleslaw. Mable was in charge of coleslaw and one of her kids dropped the biggest bowl of it getting from the car to the table. I remember thinking how odd it was to have someone here in town with all the free food at the barbecue."

"That is odd," Philo said. "Of course, as Phyllis and I decided, the car just could've been parked there. It didn't mean anyone was actually in the vicinity. Maybe the owner walked down to the barbecue."

"Was the diner open?" Laurel asked.

"Oh, yes," Phyllis said. "For passers-through and tourists. Though if they saw the signs for the barbecue, those who've got the time would come join us there instead. The car wasn't parked outside the café, though. It was several yards down the block."

Scott lifted an ankle to rest on his knee. "Has anyone said anything about noticing an unfamiliar gentleman around town? Know of anyone who might have taken him in if he got too drunk last night to make it back to Twin Oaks?"

The Coopers shook their heads in unison. "The car's gone, too."

"Did you notice when it left?"

"We didn't come back this way after the barbecue," Phyllis told him.

"She'd had a little too much of that maple candy,"

Philo said with an affectionate grin at his wife. "Her stomach was hurting her a bit."

Laurel looked over at Scott and was surprised to find that instead of watching the exchange between the older couple, he was staring at her. The look in his unusual blue eyes was unsettling.

And definitely not happy.

"You know," Philo said, diverting Laurel's attention. She looked back to see him tapping his wife on the shoulder. "Our daughter Bonnie was out at Twin Oaks yesterday. She did the plumbing on the place and had one last fixture to install in the kitchen. It had just come in late Wednesday. Maybe you ought to talk to her."

"Yeah," Phyllis said, nodding vigorously. "If there was anything out there to notice, our Bonnie would have seen it. She's a smart girl, that one."

"Bonnie became a plumber?" Laurel asked, loving the sound of that. The Coopers' daughter had been five years younger than Laurel, but she'd gotten to know Bonnie rather well during her sojourns at the grocery.

Laurel had always admired her spunk. Nothing seemed to keep Bonnie down. Even in a town as small as Cooper's Corner, she hadn't been swayed by what other people thought. She'd been as outgoing as Laurel was reserved. There'd been a time in her life when Laurel had secretly wished she *was* Bonnie Cooper.

After a couple more questions—and no more answers—Scott and Laurel left, but not before Laurel had promised to come back and have dinner with the Coopers before her vacation was over.

Odd how she wished Scott had been included in that invitation.

THE COOPERS SAID BONNIE had been called out to a plumbing emergency at the Johnsons' place that afternoon. She'd been there, but was gone. Mrs. Johnson was pretty certain Bonnie was heading over to the library to fix a leak that had sprung in the bathroom.

Scott was used to chasing around after leads, so that wasn't a problem. But having Laurel in the seat beside him was beginning to take its toll. His tolerance was wearing a little thin.

He loved having her there too much, and knew there was no hope of ever keeping her in his life—even as a friend. Eventually she was going to find out he hadn't been driving the day Paul had been killed—and why.

All of the disbelief and anger she'd spewed forth onto him the morning of the accident would spring forth again. But this time she wouldn't merely be killing the messenger. She'd be killing him.

"So Bonnie Cooper's a plumber..." she said as they drove back across town toward the library.

"Not too hard to believe, though, is it?" Scott asked. "She always was into..."

"...hardware," Laurel finished for him. "Poor Phyllis. She tried to interest Bonnie in the grocery side of the business, but all Bonnie wanted to do was play with screws and see what you could do with tools."

"You sound like you spent a lot of time at the Coopers' place," Scott said. He hadn't known that about her.

"I did. Almost every afternoon after school my freshman year. And part of my sophomore year, too. Until I started hanging out at..." She broke off.

"At our place," Scott finished for her.

"Yeah."

"I've still got the house."

"You live there alone?"

Scott nodded.

"How come you never married?" she asked quietly, staring out the front windshield. "As I recall you always had about four girls going at a time."

Scott shrugged. How did he tell her that he had nothing left to offer on a full-time basis without also telling her why?

"Guess I just never met the woman I wanted to sign on with for fifty years or more."

He had, of course. She was sitting right next to him. And that was why he'd never married.

Instead he had his work. He would be the best damn cop he could be. Contribute something to the world in the hopes that when his time came to face the final judgment, he'd have done enough good deeds to be offered some token of forgiveness for the things he'd done so horribly wrong.

Scott turned the corner, taking a shortcut to the library, and immediately wished he could turn back. Straight ahead of them, shining bright in the sun, was the pristine white church that was to have been the site of Laurel's wedding. Instead, it had been the scene of what had to have been the worst moment of her life.

Right there, in that corner of the parking lot, he'd told her that Paul was not going to make it to their wedding. Still dazed and in shock himself, he'd tried to take her in his arms, and had fought off her blows instead as she railed against him for telling her something so completely unbearable.

Scott could still feel those blows. Every single one of them.

He glanced surreptitiously sideways, wondering if he should acknowledge the building just ahead, or pretend it wasn't there. Just as they'd been pretending that Paul's death wasn't there between them, occupying both of their minds. That the pain wasn't still as fresh as it had been in that churchyard three and a half years before.

Laurel was looking out her side window, her head turned at an unnatural angle, as though she was trying to cut the church out of even her peripheral vision.

She apparently wasn't ready to talk about that day.

Scott was relieved as hell.

He wasn't ready, either.

CHAPTER FIVE

LAUREL WAS SURPRISED to get a phone call at Twin Oaks later that evening. Still dressed in the clothes she'd had on all day, she'd just finished summarizing her observations on the little handheld tape recorder that was her constant companion, and was lying in the dark on the big four-poster bed, staring out the window, trying to make sense of something.

Of anything.

Byrd's disappearance. Her feeling of homecoming in the Coopers' arms that afternoon. Scott.

And Paul. Always Paul.

Clint's son, Keegan, knocked on her door to tell her she had a call. She could take it in the office, he said.

Not sure who'd be calling her or why—except maybe the Coopers to confirm a dinner date—Laurel reluctantly left her cocoon of darkness.

Was there any point in furthering her relationship with the Coopers? It wasn't likely that she'd ever be back to Cooper's Corner again after Byrd was found.

The caller was Scott.

Laurel sank down into the roller chair behind Maureen's desk, ignoring the pleasure she felt at hearing his voice.

After following Bonnie around town that afternoon, always just missing her, Scott had finally brought Laurel back to Twin Oaks, accepting Maureen's invitation to join them all for breakfast in the morning before he and Laurel met Bonnie Cooper in town.

There'd been nothing said about any contact before then.

"Just wanted to fill you in on what I know so you have as much time to mull it over as I do," he said now, almost without preamble.

Good. That was good. "What've you got?"

"A photo of Byrd, for one. We got it from his publisher."

"That'll sure help when we're talking to people."

They'd been a bit handicapped that afternoon with only a verbal description of the man.

"Has his family been notified?"

That was something else they'd talked about late that afternoon.

"He doesn't appear to have any."

Laurel felt a new affinity for the missing man.

"I got a call back on the birth certificate."

She sat up straight. "What'd they say?"

"Leslie Renwick is the daughter of Robert and Gloria Renwick of New Bedford, Massachusetts. She lives in Worcester. I have her address."

"So why would William Byrd have her birth certificate?" Laurel asked, immediately alert.

"And why have it out at Twin Oaks?"

"Do we know if Byrd was ever married?"

"There's no record of him having married."

Again, Laurel felt a personal connection to the older man, a sense that finding him alive and well was important to her own ability to move on with her life.

"As far as I can tell, he's been living alone in Connecticut for almost thirty years. I called a private detective friend of mine to check things out in Connecticut for me—Byrd's neighbors, possible friends, his usual haunting grounds. So far, nobody's seen him.''

"So," Laurel finally said, "why would a man in his early sixties have a birth certificate for a much younger woman with the parents' names whited out?''

"My guess is when we get that answer, we'll be well on our way toward finding Byrd," Scott said.

His voice sounded a little like Paul's over the phone. Laurel had never noticed that before.

"It's highly likely that certificate had something to do with why he left in such a hurry," Laurel observed.

"There was no sign of struggle, but we should probably consider that someone could have shown up at Twin Oaks with blackmail on their mind.''

"Like maybe Byrd fathered that child, and now, thirty-five years later, someone's going to blackmail him over it?'' Laurel didn't think so.

"Hardly makes sense, does it?'' Scott said softly. "He has no family, no one to be hurt by something like that coming to light….''

"So no grounds for blackmail that we know of…''

"And even if he had fathered a child—if Leslie *was* his—why would discovering that cause him to disappear into thin air?''

"Can't think of any good reason.''

Laurel rubbed her hand across her forehead and down over her eyes. "Maybe we're completely on the wrong track here.''

"How so?''

"What if William Byrd just found that certificate—maybe sticking out from the bottom of a dresser drawer, or something? The rooms here are all furnished with antiques, a lot of them purchased during the past year. Could be somebody hid or lost that certificate years ago and Byrd just happened upon it.''

The idea might sound far-fetched, but Laurel had heard of things a lot more bizarre than that.

"That could explain why he'd just left it sitting out. He'd hardly think it was confidential if he'd found it stuck in a drawer,'' Scott said slowly.

"Good point,'' Laurel agreed. "So where does that leave us?''

"Well, since we don't have an official case, or even know for certain that we have a missing person, I can't really call Leslie Renwick and ask her if she knows why William Byrd might have a copy of her birth certificate. I guess for the time being, we assume that Byrd's finding the certificate was a fluke.''

"So we're back to square one.''

"We know he parked in town after he left Twin Oaks on Saturday,'' Scott reminded her.

"Do you think he intended to go to the barbecue and just never made it?'' She'd been so focused on that birth certificate, certain that whatever had caused Byrd to disappear had occurred at the bed-and-breakfast, that she hadn't considered any other possibility.

"Everyone at Twin Oaks heard him say he'd be there…''

Laurel started to feel slightly sick.

"…so we have to consider the possibility that…''

"Someone abducted him right there in the middle of town while everyone was down at the barbecue,'' she finished, seeming to have more control if she was the one to actually say the words rather than hear them.

"It could have happened without any outward sign of a struggle….''

"Especially if they took him in his own car.''

Scott's sigh was so deep she could almost feel the weight of it. "I have some other news."

She didn't like the sound of his voice. "What?"

"I called that bed-and-breakfast in Vermont. Byrd had a reservation there for tonight and tomorrow night. He was scheduled to arrive this afternoon."

"And he didn't."

"Nope."

Okay, well, he hadn't been back to Twin Oaks yet, either. That didn't mean…

She wasn't going to stop believing the older man was okay. "So what else have we got to go on?"

"What about the woman's negligee?" Scott asked, his voice subdued.

Staring down at the floorboards directly in front of her, Laurel hesitated before answering. "He's been alone a long time." She hated to say it. "He could just have some alternative tastes."

"Unfortunately, I can't think of a better explanation at the moment."

"If he'd had a woman here, someone would have noticed," Laurel said. "Nothing gets past Keegan." She hated where they were going with this but couldn't find a more plausible route.

"And if he'd been planning to have a woman in, why wouldn't he just say so?" Scott added. "He'd have to know that wasn't something you could keep secret in a place like Twin Oaks. So what clues does this leave us with?" he asked, sounding like he needed a good night's rest.

Laurel continued to study the pattern of floorboards in Maureen and Clint's office for a few moments. There were seven boards directly in front of her, all with varying degrees of widening grain as they approached the desk. Each board represented a clue to her.

"We have an encrypted laptop," she began.

"And a black-and-white photo of a couple getting ready to kiss," Scott added.

"Could be someone he met when he was visiting the inn on that page of the book," Laurel said.

"And they became friends..." Scott added, playing along.

"They could even be the owners."

"Maybe Leslie Renwick is their daughter." Scott's voice, while still tired, had lightened.

Laurel grinned, though it wasn't her best effort. "And they mailed him the birth certificate with their picture to include in his next book," she joked.

"I'll see you in the morning," Scott said, his voice leaving her warmer than she'd felt all evening.

"Okay," she answered as softly, intimately.

And then, with leaded feet, she headed back upstairs, feeling guilty for taking from Scott, even in the smallest measure, the comfort she used to get from Paul.

She'd hoped she was ready to move on, but was beginning to fear she'd end up just like William Byrd— alone for the rest of her life.

In love with a memory.

HALF AN HOUR LATER, Keegan knocked on Laurel's door a second time and she headed back downstairs to the office. Expecting to hear Scott's voice telling her he'd thought of something else, Laurel couldn't figure out for a second who was the owner of the male voice on the other end of the line.

"Laurel?" the man asked again. His voice was warm.

Familiar. Concerned. ''I just got your message. Are you okay?''

Shane. Her heart dropped. Right along with her shoulders and her spirits. Other than leaving a brief message on Shane's voice mail telling him she wouldn't be returning as soon as she'd expected, she hadn't given a thought to the gorgeous, rich and available newscaster back in New York.

''I'm fine,'' she told him, thinking the words were partially true. She hadn't fallen apart. In some ways she was handling her return to Cooper's Corner much better than she'd expected.

What she hadn't expected was to have him call her here. They didn't have that kind of relationship. At least not yet.

''I got your message.''

''Oh. Good.'' Shouldn't she be telling him about the thoughts and feelings that had been plaguing her so much earlier in the evening? Shouldn't she tell him about meeting the Coopers again—and Scott? Shane knew that's why she'd come back to Cooper's Corner—to try to resolve the past and move forward into the future, a future he wanted to share with her.

If this was the man she was going to consider developing an exclusive relationship with—the first man she'd even considered dating since Paul's death—why couldn't she at least talk to him about the wars raging inside her?

''I was worried,'' he said.

''No need.'' Laurel had always been private, keeping to herself—until she'd met Paul. And then, only with him and his family had she felt safe enough to open up a little bit.

''You're finding the stay restful?''

''I'm actually working on a possible story.'' Come to

think of it, she realized, even after a three-and-a-half year separation, she'd given Scott more this afternoon than she was able to give Shane now.

Laurel's head started to ache. Of course, talking to Scott was natural, considering the history they shared. The grief they shared.

"What story?" Shane asked. If he'd sounded resentful—or jealous—Laurel wouldn't have had such a hard time. Instead he sounded concerned, like the friend he'd grown to be these past months, and that made her feel even guiltier for her inability to share herself with him.

"One of the guests—a man in his early sixties—disappeared from Twin Oaks on Saturday. As a favor to the owners here, a state policeman is conducting an unofficial investigation on his own time. He's letting me join him."

"Any leads?"

"Nothing conclusive, yet," she told him.

He asked a couple more questions, all of which she answered generally.

"So...how'd the rest of the trip go?"

She knew exactly what he was asking. What he was waiting to hear. "Fine." At that moment, Laurel truly hated herself. What was it with her? Was she buried so deeply inside herself she could no longer open up even when she wanted to?

"Have you seen anyone you knew?"

Briefly Laurel told him about the elder Coopers. And because she felt so bad knowing that she wasn't going to tell him about Scott—and even worse because she didn't understand why—she went on to tell him about Bonnie, too, and her plumbing career.

As she talked—and made Shane laugh—Laurel relaxed a bit, but only enough to get through the rest of the conversation. Before hanging up, she promised Shane that she'd call him when she got back to New York.

And then she went upstairs to bed. She knew she would have trouble sleeping, so she poured herself a glass of wine from the bottle she'd brought with her.

Although she didn't drink a lot, there'd been many nights after the accident when a glass of wine was the only thing that helped her ease up enough to get some sleep.

But tonight the wine didn't do the trick, and she lay awake, staring out at the impenetrable darkness of the country night, and wondering if she was ever going to know who she was or where she was going.

"YOU'RE GOING TO LOVE my dad's griddle cakes," Keegan told Scott the next morning at the huge mahogany table in the dining room. Though the chintz-covered chairs were simple cottage-style, they were surprisingly comfortable.

"I've heard a lot about them," Scott said, smiling at the solidly built boy who'd waited until Scott sat down and then plopped into the seat next to him.

Scott had just come in from filling Clint and Maureen in on the little bit of progress they'd made on Byrd's case. He'd been in touch with Frank Quigg, Maureen's former boss at the NYPD. Apparently Owen Nevil was on a hiking expedition and could not be reached.

The brother-and-sister team were getting ready to welcome the next batch of guests to Twin Oaks. Three families were due to arrive that afternoon and were staying for a couple of days.

"Hi!"

"Are you the…"

"…policeman we seed sometimes?"

Scott blinked, and turned to see the two identical curly-headed girls who'd just tromped in to stand beside the table and stare up at him. He'd seen the twins around town a time or two, but never up close.

"That one's Robin and that's Randi," Keegan informed him.

"Girls, come get in your seats," Maureen said, having entered the room right behind them.

"Yes," Scott said as the pair immediately left his side to climb into a couple of booster seats across the table from him. "I am a policeman."

"Did you know Mommy?" one of the little girls asked. Like her sister, she was wearing a pink T-shirt that read I'm An Angel across the front.

Scott believed the pronouncement.

"In New York?" the other little girl asked.

"No." Scott shook his head just as Maureen reminded the girls that they weren't supposed to talk about Mommy's job in New York.

"He's from Cooper's Corner, dummies," Keegan added, glancing apologetically at Scott.

Scott's heart went out to the boy. He was at that tough age where he was too old to be a kid, too young to be a man, and aware of both.

Laurel came in and sat down next to Maureen and her girls rather than Scott. She wasn't meeting his eyes that morning. He wondered if she'd changed her mind about the investigation and was planning to head back to New York.

And did not approve—at all—of how much he hoped that wasn't the case.

Clint joined them at the table, and Scott soon found that everything he'd heard about Clint's griddle cakes was true. He was afforded the opportunity to enjoy them without interruption as the twins kept up a steady dialogue. Amused himself, Scott noticed how entranced Laurel seemed to be with the pair.

"Mommy's goin' to let us run in the hose!" announced Robin.

"Just as soon as breakfast is done!" chimed in Randi.

Laurel's eyes danced as she gazed from one twin to the next. "And who's going to count to ten before you start?" she asked, as though she was aware of their routine.

"We are!" both girls shouted.

"But I betcha can't count to twenty," she challenged, taking a bite of melon. The rest of them didn't need to be in the room for all the attention she was paying them.

"Yes we can!" the girls cried. "One, two, three, four..." They made it all the way to twenty.

Their mother and uncle grinned with pride from either end of the table.

"You gotta admit, they *are* pretty smart," Keegan leaned over to whisper. He'd filled his plate with everything from the buffet — his father's griddle cakes, sausage, bacon, eggs, a croissant and hash browns.

"That they are," Scott whispered back.

"Girls, eat your eggs," Maureen said. She was apparently just having an English muffin for breakfast.

The girls each took a bite, though it took one of them—Scott had lost track of who was who—a few tries to get the scrambled eggs to her mouth. They kept falling off her spoon. He almost laughed out loud when she finally just picked up the glob of eggs with her fingers and shoved it in.

"We can count to forty, too!" one of the girls told Laurel.

"Show me."

Laurel was great with the twins, Scott realized. And

had she married his brother on the day intended, she would very probably be teaching her own son or daughter to count rather than coaxing numbers out of virtual strangers.

The thought saddened him enough to curb his appetite.

CHAPTER SIX

"YOU LOOK NICE TODAY."

"Thanks." Climbing into Scott's Blazer as he held the door for her, Laurel felt a rush of purely feminine pleasure. There was absolutely nothing spectacular about the white stretch denim slacks she was wearing, or the short-sleeved cotton top, but he made her feel as though there was.

On vacation now, he was out of uniform and dressed in gray slacks and a white button-down shirt with the sleeves rolled up. She'd never before been moved by a man with rolled up sleeves. It must be his resemblance to Paul that was affecting her now.

"I had a friend of mine from crisis training make a visit to William's neighborhood in Connecticut," he told her.

Her heart leapt. "And?"

"Nothing. Apparently he comes and goes a lot, so being away for an extended time is nothing out of the ordinary."

Laurel had a feeling she'd better prepare herself for a slew of disappointments over the next day or two.

As previously arranged, they met Bonnie Cooper at her home—a former cottage she owned in town.

With her maple-brown eyes and milk-chocolate hair, Bonnie was just as Laurel remembered her. A little taller, maybe, but still wearing her infectious smile and offering the small-town welcome that seemed to be part of everyone who'd ever lived in Cooper's Corner.

"It's so good to see you!" Bonnie said, giving Laurel a strong hug.

"You, too," Laurel replied, grinning for a moment in spite of the serious reason for their visit. Dressed in denim overalls and a ribbed T-shirt, Bonnie looked young and cute.

Fun-loving. Just as Laurel remembered her.

She offered them a cup of coffee and the three of them settled at the kitchen table.

She didn't have much information for them in the Byrd case.

"He wasn't at the B and B when I was there on Saturday afternoon," she said. "I was the only one in the house—everyone else was at the barbecue."

"You're sure his car wasn't in the drive?" Scott asked, his notebook out.

"Positive," she said. "I pulled my truck all the way around back. I didn't want anyone to know where I was and ask me to do any more jobs that were going to keep me from getting to the barbecue—and there were no other cars back there." She frowned. "Why?"

"He's missing," Laurel gently told the other woman.

Bonnie instantly stilled, lowering the half-raised cup she held back to its saucer. "Missing?" she repeated.

Scott and Laurel nodded.

"He hasn't been seen since Saturday morning," Scott said.

"That's two days ago!"

A twinge of fear shot through Laurel, a reaction to the concern she read in the other woman's expressive eyes.

They were going to find William Byrd. Alive. She was certain of it.

But she would feel a whole lot better if she knew the older man hadn't been the victim of foul play.

If someone had hurt him...

Since there was nothing more Bonnie could tell them, Scott directed the conversation back to Bonnie's specialty—restoration plumbing. She was the best source in the area for authentic hardware and vintage fixtures.

"How'd you get into plumbing?" Laurel asked Bonnie as the three walked out a few minutes later. "All you ever talked about was teaching at Theodore Cooper Elementary."

Bonnie chuckled. "I had a bit of an idealized vision of being a teacher. I mean, look at Cooper Elementary—it's so picturesque it could be on a postcard. I always imagined wearing horn-rimmed glasses and plaid outfits, and having dozens of little darlings bringing me apples."

"So what happened?"

"Teaching my first class."

Laurel laughed out loud at the look of chagrin on Bonnie's face.

"Too hot for you to handle, eh, Bonnie?" Scott asked with a grin.

"Bite me, Hunter."

Laurel envied the easy grin the two of them shared, and their relaxed way with each other, almost as though they were brother and sister.

That's what living in a small town could do, she remembered. Give you the illusion that you really did have a family to call your own.

"So you chose plumbing because it was the furthest thing from teaching?" Laurel asked, charmed as always, by the younger woman. Bonnie liked plain food, plain talk and country music. Laurel had expected her to be married with babies by now, not traipsing off in overalls fixing people's toilets.

"No," Bonnie chuckled. "During high school I learned to do simple installations while helping Dad out at the store. It was a good way to earn some extra money. And it didn't take me long to figure out that the more I knew, the more money I made. I registered as an apprentice when I went to college and worked my way through a bachelor's degree."

"She's damn good," Scott told Laurel. "Makes quite a name for herself helping the city people who move to the area and want to build period homes."

"I'm actually still working to be a journeyman," Bonnie admitted. "But I think I've found my niche with the restoration stuff. Nothing like finding just the right ball cock."

"What?" Laurel choked.

"You know, ball…cock. Think about it." Scott sent her a grin he shouldn't be sending. One that made Laurel's cheeks burn and her heart beat faster.

He's not Paul, she reminded herself. And then turned cold.

Were loneliness and grief driving her to transfer her love for Paul to his younger brother? God, she hoped not. Really hoped not.

She'd guard against it with her life.

"Shut up, Hunter," Bonnie said. And after sending Scott a disgusted look, she turned to Laurel. "A ball cock's an automatic valve—its opening and closing are controlled by the float at the end of the flush lever on toilets," Bonnie explained.

Scott had known that. He'd been teasing her. Like in the old days.

Laurel suddenly felt like crying.

"DID YOU EVER GO OUT with Bonnie Cooper?"

Scott didn't like the pleasure Laurel's question brought him—as though she actually cared about whom he did and didn't date.

"No."

They'd left the younger woman a couple of hours before and had spent the rest of the morning showing Byrd's picture around town, to no avail. Not that Scott was surprised. Most everyone in Cooper's Corner had been at the barbecue on Saturday.

"You dated a lot in high school, though," Laurel said. She was looking out her window. He couldn't see her expression.

He had no reason to take hope that she was at all interested in his love life. Laurel was in love with his dead brother. There was no future for her with Scott, because Paul's memory still lived on in her heart, and Paul's death weighed heavily on his.

"I don't think I dated any more than anyone else," Scott replied eventually.

"Yeah," Laurel said, her voice taking on that half condescending, half teasing tone that shot straight to his groin. "If I went out with even a quarter as many guys as you did girls, I'd have been considered a sleaze. And would have failed school, too."

"You're hardly a qualified judge of such things," Scott told her. "You only dated one guy your whole life."

He could have bitten off his tongue for bringing Paul into the conversation. And yet, maybe what he'd done was exactly right.

Paul was going to keep him safe. From her. From himself.

"In high school, I guess you're right," Laurel said slowly.

"You dated other guys in college? I know you went to different schools, but I thought you and Paul were exclusive even then."

"We were." Her voice sounded far away. "But Paul's been gone for three and a half years."

Scott's blood ran cold. "Are you seeing someone?" The idea had never occurred to him, though it should have.

Of course Laurel would be dating. She was young. Beautiful. She had her whole life ahead of her. A husband. Kids.

"No," she said.

He knew he was in trouble when that single word brought a flood of relief. He had to find Byrd and get this woman out of his life once and for all before he did something he'd regret for the rest of his life.

Like make a move on his dead brother's fiancée.

"Not at all?" He'd told himself not to ask.

"No."

She'd loved Paul that much.

"You ever going to?"

"I hope so." She didn't sound sure.

Driving back up to Twin Oaks for afternoon tea and to make some calls, Scott forced himself to face facts.

Laurel was still in love with Paul.

And Scott was still a sick son of a bitch—in love with his older brother's woman.

THAT EVENING, FRUSTRATED and verging on terse, Scott moved with Laurel from table to table at Tubb's Café, showing William Byrd's picture to everyone there.

No one had seen Byrd.

As impossible as it seemed, the man had simply vanished. He sure as hell hoped that the fact that Owen Nevil was also absent was a complete coincidence.

"Isn't that Seth Castleman?" Laurel whispered, pointing to a lone figure in a booth in the back of the café.

Scott followed the direction of her finger. Seth was only six years younger than he was, yet Scott barely recognized the man as the person he'd grown up with. Nowadays the electrician seemed afflicted with a terrible, terminal sadness. "Yep, that's him," he said quietly. The life might have gone out of Seth, but there was no mistaking Castleman's muscular build, not in these parts.

"He had the most unusual eyes," Laurel said, walking slowly toward the booth. "Almost amber."

Scott wouldn't know about that.

He just knew he didn't like the way Laurel seemed to gravitate to the other man. Didn't like knowing full well that Castleman was free to pursue Laurel if he ever chose to.

Not like Scott, who could only love her from far, too far away. Who really couldn't love her at all.

One kiss. If he could only have one taste of those lips...

He was crossing a line he should not cross. One he swore he'd never cross.

"Is he still single?" Laurel asked.

"Yes." Scott was no longer just verging on terseness.

"It's such a shame," she said softly. "Has anyone heard anything from Wendy?"

Wendy Monroe was one of Cooper's Corner's claims to fame. A skier of champion status, she'd left town to fly to Europe to participate in her first Olympics—left her fiancé, Seth Castleman, at home to watch her on national television. But she'd never made it to the television screen. At least not on the slopes. The week before the Olympics, in a practice run, she'd had an accident, hit a tree and ended up paralyzed. The doctors thought she'd have to spend the rest of her life in a wheelchair.

Seth had flown to Europe immediately, and two weeks later he'd come back. Alone. He'd been alone ever since.

"Bonnie was telling me a few months ago that Wendy's walking again," Scott said now.

Bonnie and Seth and Wendy had all gone to school together. They'd been good friends.

"You're kidding!" Laurel said, stopping Scott with a hand on his forearm. She stared at him. "They said she'd never get out of that chair."

"Wendy's one determined lady."

"Is she skiing?" Laurel asked, glancing back at Seth.

Scott shook his head. "I don't think so. Apparently she has quite a limp."

"You think he still loves her?"

"I don't know," Scott answered honestly. "I hope not."

But he didn't really hold out much hope. Cooper's Corner seemed to breed lifelong love, unrequited or not.

Look at him, still loving Laurel, and Laurel so much in love with Paul.

Hell yeah, of course Castleman still loved Wendy Monroe. Poor fool.

"YEAH, I SAW HIM," Castleman said when Scott showed him Byrd's photo.

With an urgency he'd been itching to feel all day, Scott handed the photo to Laurel and reached for his notebook.

"When? Where?" Laurel asked.

Scott didn't have time to bother with the appreciation he recognized in the younger man's eyes as Seth looked at Laurel. He didn't have time. But he was bothered.

"In here. Saturday afternoon."

Scott and Laurel exchanged glances.

"He was with some woman," Seth continued, taking a bite of his home-style meat loaf.

"Can you describe her?" Scott asked.

"Slender, nicely dressed, average height. Mid to late fifties."

Scott looked up from his notebook. "Gray hair?"

Nodding, Seth said, "Silver. I didn't see her up close so guess I can't say for the record who she was," he admitted, "but at the time I was certain she was the widow who bought the Wallace place outside of New Ashford. She's using it for a summer home. I did some work out there shortly after she bought the place, but I only met her once. Most of my dealings were with the Realtor."

New Ashford was Cooper's Corner's neighboring village, and the Wallace place, while beautiful, was well-known only in that it had once been owned by a famous ballet dancer, and then later, an eccentric artist, neither of whom visited often. Mostly the property stood vacant.

"You're pretty sure it was her, though?" Scott asked.

"Unofficially?"

Scott nodded.

"I'm certain it was. I don't remember her name, though. The realty company paid my bill."

Taking a seat in a vacant booth, Scott pulled out his cell phone and made some calls to find out the name of the woman who'd recently purchased the Wallace place, while Laurel ordered cranberry cobbler and sodas for both of them.

"Any luck?" she asked as he switched off his phone.

"None. Everyone's gone home. We'll have to wait till morning."

"Should we drive out there? Take a look around?"

Scott shook his head. "It's not like we'd be able to see anything in the dark, and until we have an ID on the woman, I'd rather not knock on any doors. Not yet, anyway."

Laurel gave him an encouraging smile. "It's less than twelve hours until morning...."

She was right, of course. Still, it was another day further away from Byrd's safe return. Crime statistics showed pretty conclusively that the longer the man was missing, the less his chances of being found unharmed.

SCOTT WAS FROWNING. Laurel had to stop herself from reaching over and smoothing her finger along that furrowed brow—an action she'd done to Paul hundreds of times as he'd studied or concentrated on a law brief.

So many times in the past three and a half years she'd regretted letting Paul, her dear, conservative, conscientious lover, talk her into waiting until he passed the bar exam and become established in a firm before they got married. Having to support himself, he'd taken longer than most to get through school, and hadn't been satisfied with just a junior position in a law firm. It wouldn't have paid enough to support her and pay off his school loans. He'd had some sweet notion about not having her support him through school, though she'd have been very happy to do so.

She wished now she'd insisted on it.

She wouldn't be sitting there seeing him in his younger brother if she had. Wouldn't be thinking she wanted Scott, when it was really Paul she longed for.

"How do you do it?" She probably shouldn't ask, but spending so much time with Scott in the past two days had given her a false sense of emotional closeness.

"Do what?" He was bent slightly over his cobbler, though he wasn't eating the dessert with any relish.

"Get by," she said, setting her fork down on a plate still half-full. "Keep going."

He glanced up, the look in his blue eyes tired but piercing. "Who says I do?"

"Don't you?"

"Some days, maybe."

"And on those days when you don't get by, what do you do then?"

"Work."

Laurel, too. All the time. Work was her salvation. Her life. The keeper of her sanity.

"Do you ever get mad?"

He frowned, putting a bite into his mouth with deliberation and chewing slowly. "Sure."

"At God for taking him?"

"Maybe. Occasionally." He wasn't meeting her eyes.

"At Paul?"

"No."

Laurel swallowed a lump of guilt. "Never?"

"Never." He glanced up then. "Do you?"

She didn't know what to say. She couldn't lie to him, but was ashamed to tell him the truth.

"Sometimes." She blinked back tears that didn't come as readily these days as they had during that first year. "I just get so mad at him for not hanging on, for letting fate take him away, for not choosing to stay with me...."

Scott didn't say anything, but his gaze was warm, not disgusted.

"Crazy, huh?" Laurel asked.

"No." He shook his head and took another slow bite of cobbler, almost as if it were his duty to clean his plate, not because he actually wanted the dessert. "Anger is a perfectly natural phase of grief."

She knew that. She'd learned it in her Life After Loss classes. "But it's been three and a half years. That phase should have ended by now."

"You still get mad at him?"

"Yeah."

"You mad at him right now?"

His gaze held hers, leaving Laurel feeling confused— and yet more alive than she'd felt since she'd left this town devastated and unable to cope three and a half years ago.

"Maybe," she said. "A little." And then, after a long pause, "Yes. A lot."

Scott reached across and covered her hand where it was resting on the table. "It's okay, you know."

Afraid she was going to cry, Laurel nodded.

"Being back here, remembering, it's natural that you'd relive it all."

He made her sound so normal.

"It's just that I've tried so hard," she said. "I really thought I was ready to come home...come back here," she corrected. Cooper's Corner was not home to her. It couldn't be. It was hell on earth—it represented all she'd dared to reach out for, only to have it cruelly snatched away.

But it was certainly the most beautiful, welcoming hell she'd ever known.

"I thought I was finally healing."

"So why are you so sure you aren't?"

"Because." She couldn't tell him—couldn't tell anyone, but most of all not him.

"Because why?" His voice was soft, coaxing, his thumb rubbing gently across the top of her hand.

"I can't tell you." The words were almost a whisper.

"You can tell me anything, Laurel. You used to. We were almost related, for God's sake. You're the only family I've got left." He paused, and then said quietly, "After all we've been through, we've earned the right to confide in each other, haven't we?"

Tears swam in her eyes, blurring her vision, but Laurel couldn't look away from him. She'd had no problem keeping everyone else in her life at bay these past three and a half years. For the past lifetime.

What was it about the Hunter men—about Scott—that kept calling out to her?

An affinity born of grief?

"I'm angry because every time I look at you I feel things that I shouldn't be feeling," she confessed. "At least not for you."

His gaze took on a glint she'd never seen before. There was no danger in it, yet her heart started to beat such a furious tattoo she could feel its reverberation.

"What things?"

Licking lips that were uncomfortably dry, Laurel knew she shouldn't tell him. But she couldn't not tell him.

"Things I should only be feeling for Paul. Things I would be feeling for Paul if he hadn't taken the easy way out and left me here to deal with life all alone...."

Scott didn't say anything, but his grip on her hand tightened.

Things had just changed between them.

CHAPTER SEVEN

SCOTT DIDN'T SLEEP MUCH that night.

After dropping Laurel off at Twin Oaks—obsessed with kissing her good-night and equally obsessed with *not* kissing her good-night, he'd gone home to the house he'd once shared with Paul and his father, and he could hardly stand being with himself.

He was in love with his brother's woman. And she'd just opened the door to the possibility of a more intimate relationship between them.

He alternated between thinking he should have said something when she'd given him the chance, and hating a life that had taken away his right to do so. She was "feeling things" for him.

They couldn't be anything like the "things" he'd been feeling for her for almost half his life.

But there could be nothing between them. Not now. Not ever. Scott was supposed to have been his brother's keeper. Instead, he'd been his killer.

Sometime in the middle of the night, he forced himself to go to bed. But when he finally drifted off, he got even less rest than when he'd been awake.

Scott wasn't a dreaming man, but that night his sleep was filled with big black dogs. He'd fight them off, performing amazing martial arts kicks and blocking vicious jaws with his arm; he'd see them lying flat in an alley. He'd move on to something else, be somewhere else, and black dogs would be there, too. Always coming at him. He could slay them again and again, but he could never be free of them.

He awoke early the next morning to a ringing telephone. It was his friend calling to give him the name of the woman who'd bought the Wallace place. Cecilia Hamilton. His buddy didn't know too much more about her yet, except that she was the sole buyer and had no police record. And she had a personalized license plate that read "remember."

With the phone still to his ear, Scott pulled a pair of slacks and a shirt from his closet. It might be earlier than he normally started his day when he was on vacation, but he was grateful to get up and escape the dreams haunting him.

Knowing that Clint was up early to start breakfast for the guests, he rang Twin Oaks as soon as he'd shaved and showered. If Laurel was still in bed, he'd catch up with her later in the morning.

Scott needed to get to work.

MS. CECILIA HAMILTON WAS not at home that morning. Or at least she wasn't answering her phone.

Hoping she'd gone out to breakfast and would be home soon, Scott stopped for Laurel—who'd been up early, too—and the two of them headed to New Ashford.

"Remember the ice-cream store in New Ashford?" Laurel asked. It was the first thing she'd said since climbing into the car.

"Seeing that I was just there last week, yeah, I remember it."

She turned in the seat. "It's still there?" Scott could feel those amazing gray eyes on him.

He didn't want to feel them.

Didn't want to notice how her skintight black pants hugged her thighs, or how sexy that white T-shirt looked, pulled taut across her breasts.

But apparently they'd both reached the same conclusion about the night before—pretend she'd never said what she did.

"It's not only still there," he told her, forcing himself to think cold thoughts. "It's exactly the same as it was when we were in high school."

"With the red vinyl stools and Formica counter?"

"And the spot on the wall where you carved your and Paul's initials."

"He was really mad."

Scott had forgotten that.

"And you apologized," Scott remembered the rest. That apology had made him really angry at Laurel—and at Paul.

"Of course I did."

"There's no 'of course' about it. You did nothing wrong. The shop put the wooden panel in just for that purpose. Those carvings are part of its charm."

"But you know how Paul was," Laurel said softly. Scott hated the jealousy that shot through him at the tenderness in her voice.

After all, hadn't she been telling him just last night that the "things" she was feeling were really for Paul?

"Too uptight for his own good sometimes." Scott couldn't believe he was speaking ill of his dead brother. Couldn't believe he was even *thinking* ill of him. Was this woman doing this to him? Making him so crazy for her that he'd betray Paul again?

"He just walked a straight-and-narrow path," Laurel said. There was no defensiveness in her voice, only compassion.

Scott was pretty sure he'd have preferred defensiveness. Then maybe he could get angry. He drove silently, concentrating on not saying anything else he'd regret.

"He might have seemed overly conservative to some people," Laurel continued after a time. "But he was just what I needed."

"You were fifteen when you met him."

"Yeah."

"Not usually an age when a girl knows just what she needs for the rest of her life."

"I wasn't your average girl."

Of course she wasn't. She was an angel come to earth.

But that wasn't what she meant. "That's right. You were starved for love." Guilt seized Scott as soon as the words left his mouth. "I know you loved Paul, but you also loved being loved. Admit it."

He didn't know why he was doing this. Why pushing her was so important. But after all these years of loving her, of silently swallowing the frustration, the hurt, the things that he'd needed out of love and concern to say, he could no longer keep silent. He'd never be able to love her as he needed to. His own conscience wasn't going to allow that, even if by some miracle she suddenly woke up and found herself in love with him.

But...

"I loved being loved." She was looking out her window and the words were muffled.

"You never looked at another guy after you met Paul. And you were only fifteen," he repeated. "How do you know there wasn't someone out there who was even more perfect for you than Paul was? Someone who wasn't going to curtail every spontaneous impulse you had?"

"I wasn't spontaneous! I've never been spontaneous.

When it comes to my personal life I'm the most cautious person I've ever known.''

''And when you finally had a family to love you, when you started to trust us to be there for you, that person who'd been locked defensively inside you during all those years of being shuffled from one foster family to the next started to emerge.''

She made a sound. Scott waited, thinking she'd said something. But maybe not.

''That girl had an infectious spontaneity Laurel. Not that it had much chance to take root. Paul squelched it fairly rapidly.''

''I needed Paul,'' she said, her voice taking on an edge it hadn't had before. A certainty. ''I needed his conservativeness, his unwavering ability to stick to the road he was on.''

''Because his road led to you?''

He could understand that. He just didn't like it. That was no reason to tie herself to someone—and now to his memory—for the rest of her life.

''No,'' she said, slowly turning to face him. ''Because I needed someone who would teach me to trust. Someone who was going to be predictable, who I could count on to do exactly what he said he was going to do, someone who wasn't going to change his mind about me. Someone I could believe.''

As a child she'd been told so many times that she was home—only to be taken away again when the family decided they no longer wanted to do foster care, or the money wasn't enough to make the job worthwhile anymore. Or when they got pregnant with a child of their own and needed Laurel's room.

Scott knew all of those things had happened to her.

''What about now?'' He had to ask—to twist his own

knife a little deeper, give those demons inside him more reason to keep tormenting him. "Do you still think you need someone conservative like Paul?"

"I still love Paul."

It didn't quite answer the question he'd asked.

Or maybe it did.

CECILIA HAMILTON'S HOME was a beautiful ranch-style building with a huge expanse of lawn broken only by the occasional flower bed filled with colorful, late-blooming perennials.

Those flower beds were well tended. Someone had to be in residence, or a service had been hired to care for the place.

"And this is a summer home?" Laurel said, accompanying Scott up the massive walk.

He grinned. "Kind of makes you wonder what her real home looks like, doesn't it?"

There was no answer to Scott's knock on the front door.

"Maybe she's out for the morning," Laurel said, peeking in the curtained front window.

"And maybe she returned to her full-time residence."

"Before the end of summer?"

"Let's check around back." She was standing too close to him. He was smelling lilacs again.

Though he made no reply, he followed Laurel as she rounded the corner of Ms. Hamilton's home.

"Oh, my God." Her voice shook.

Alarmed, Scott stopped. "What?"

She pointed. He looked.

And froze.

William Byrd's car was in the driveway.

SCOTT'S PACE QUICKENED. He pulled the notebook out of his pocket, though he didn't need it. He'd already ascertained that the license on the black BMW matched the one Byrd had left on his registration at Twin Oaks.

"So he was with her," Laurel said, looking in the passenger side of the car as Scott tried the driver's door.

The car was locked.

"Apparently."

"But if his car's here, why isn't he?" Cupping her hands around her face to shield the light, Laurel peered in the back window. "There's nothing in the car."

Scott made note of the mileage on the odometer. "Let's go try the house again."

Their second attempt was no more successful than the first. Pulling out his cell phone, Scott tried Ms. Hamilton's number again.

Nothing.

If someone was home, they were choosing not to let anyone know.

"LOOK AT THIS," LAUREL SAID, pulling newspapers out of a delivery slot by the front door. She was getting a bad feeling about this whole thing and was very glad that Scott was with her. "There are over three days' worth of papers here."

"That pretty well indicates she didn't plan to be away," Scott said.

"Or else she'd have canceled the paper," Laurel finished for him.

Scott took the newsprint from her. "They date back to Saturday."

"She wasn't here then, but Byrd's car was?"

"Or it came later."

Laurel frowned. "Do you think William's been here without her?"

"It's possible."

"Maybe when they met for lunch, she gave him a key to the place." Laurel desperately wanted to hope so.

"Maybe. Doesn't make sense that he'd stay here without first getting his stuff from Twin Oaks, though."

"Especially since his computer was there."

She'd never noticed how stern Scott looked when he was focused on an idea. For that matter, she'd never noticed such intense concentration in him before. He'd always seemed more interested in getting her and Paul to lighten up.

But he was the smartest man she'd ever met. Scott had a photographic memory, and all through high school he'd never studied for a test, yet graduated with a perfect grade point.

Since they were alone, Laurel pulled out her tape recorder and chronicled a few of her observations—more for descriptive purposes than for solving the case.

"Makes you wonder if someone was really after Cecilia Hamilton," Scott said, taking up the conversation as if they'd been talking right along. He was checking windowsills and bushes.

"And William just got caught in the middle of things." She hated to even say the words. William Byrd was not in that kind of trouble. He was not going to be the innocent victim in someone else's game.

"I'm going to check around some more," Scott said.

Laurel followed him, partly because she, too, wanted more of a look around. Two sets of eyes were better than one, and they might find some fresh footprints or a matchbox or key ring someone dropped.

She also followed because at the moment, being with Scott made her feel better than standing out in front of the house without him.

Ms. HAMILTON'S GARAGE was empty.

Laurel's instincts were telling her that they were on to something serious.

"Do you think someone could have been after William and took Ms. Hamilton, too?" she asked.

"Of course it's a possibility. And maybe someone was after both of them—or neither of them, and they just happened to be in the wrong place at the wrong time."

"One thing's for sure," she said, following Scott back out to his car. "It doesn't make sense that they're just happily off someplace together, or Byrd would have checked out of Twin Oaks."

"Or at least called."

"So whatever happened to Mr. Byrd, it's serious enough to have prevented him from getting back to the bed-and-breakfast."

"For several days."

Laurel buckled herself into the front seat next to Scott. It was beginning to feel like her seat. Like she belonged.

And as much as she liked that, she didn't like it at all.

It wasn't fair to Scott, this dependency she was developing on him. She was transferring her grief for Paul into a need to be close to his younger brother. And it wasn't healthy for her to be feeling such peace inside when she was with Scott.

Scott pulled into the driveway next door to Cecilia Hamilton's. "I'm going up to ask a few questions," he said, giving her a sideways glance. He hadn't looked her straight in the eye all morning. "You want to wait here?"

"Not unless you need me to."

"No." He didn't hesitate. "You're welcome to come along."

Laurel was out of the Blazer before he was.

As it turned out, they questioned several of the neighbors and found out very little.

Though they'd all met Cecilia at an open house they'd held to welcome her to the neighborhood, no one had seen her much since then. They'd had a get-together barbecue and swim on Saturday on the terrace of one of the mammoth homes, but Cecilia never arrived.

She drove a white Crown Victoria, and no one had even seen that since Saturday morning.

Back in the Blazer, Scott called a buddy of his at work and asked him to let Scott know if anyone reported Ms. Hamilton's car abandoned. Then he backed up to Ms. Hamilton's driveway again.

"I want to check around one more time," he told Laurel. She followed him, wondering what he was looking for, but not wanting to ask while he was so focused.

Scott was a lot more aggressive in his search this time, checking windows, working around the security system— something he seemed quite adept at—so he could test for an unlocked window or loose door latch. He stopped just short of picking a lock or breaking the door down. Technically he should have waited to get a warrant, but without an official investigation, that wasn't possible.

And lives might be at stake.

THEY LEARNED ONE THING MORE about Cecilia Hamilton: her house was very secure. The elaborate security system was only the beginning. She had dead bolts on all of her windows and doors, and, Scott told Laurel, probably sensors, as well. When it became obvious that he wasn't going to get inside, and he'd exhausted his search of the premises outdoors, they finally gave up and headed back to Cooper's Corner. On the way, Scott tossed Laurel his notebook and had her read back to him everything that he'd written.

Laurel began reading his notes in a professional voice—until she reached the part where he'd written her name. More than once. With heavy lead.

She skipped that part, but she couldn't ignore what she'd seen.

And the thought of Scott writing her name like that made it hard for her to breathe.

SCOTT MADE A FEW CALLS, including one to William's publisher to see if they knew anything about the author's whereabouts or whom he associated with. But the people he needed to speak to were out until the next morning, so all he could do was wait to hear back on the various calls he had out.

That was the part of his job Scott hated the most.

He should take Laurel back to Twin Oaks, but he knew he wasn't going to do that. He couldn't bear to waste whatever hours or days he had left with her before she was gone from his life for good.

And because he didn't trust himself, he figured it was probably time to tell her the truth about some things. Paul's death—maybe. His own wrongful feelings— maybe. He couldn't imagine confessing any of it. Yet he knew he was going to have to tell Laurel he wasn't the man she thought he was.

That look in her eyes the previous night had really undone him. He'd spent more than half of his life wanting just a single glimpse of that look directed at him, and yet he knew that he could never, *ever*, pursue the desire he'd read there.

"Have you had a chance to spend any time out in the

country since you've been here?'' he asked, craving the peace and freedom of the Berkshire countryside.

''Just driving. I didn't feel comfortable walking around alone....''

Scott grinned. ''This is Cooper's Corner, not New York City.''

''I know. I should've gone.''

''So let's stop by Tubb's Café for some sandwiches and drive down by the old sugar bush for a picnic,'' he said as they reached the outskirts of town and she'd said nothing about seeing him at all the rest of the day.

''Okay.''

If she'd had any idea of even half the content of his thoughts, she wouldn't have agreed so easily.

She wouldn't have agreed at all.

CHAPTER EIGHT

IN BUSINESS FOR ALMOST a hundred years, Smith's Maple Sugar Bush was a family-owned sugarhouse that was pretty much a monument in that part of the Berkshires. The stand of old maples turned to a blaze of fiery colors in the fall, and in the summer provided welcome shade from the hot sun. During their high school years, the sugar bush and its surrounding meadow had been the site of more than one weekend party—parties that lasted from Saturday afternoon until Sunday morning. Kids would bring sleeping bags, build a bonfire, and tell scary stories, and as long as there was no alcohol and they cleaned up after they left, the Smith family didn't mind.

Scott remembered those times with fondness. He hoped he'd still remember the sugar bush with such fondness after this afternoon.

"This is so good," Laurel said, biting into a chicken salad sandwich. "Just like one your grandma might make."

He wondered how Laurel could make such associations when she'd never had a grandma.

He wondered if she'd ever be one.

Scott ate silently, enjoying the sandwiches, chips and fruit as though this were going to be his last supper.

In a way, he felt it was.

"Where do you picture yourself five years from now?"

he asked, propped up on one elbow on the blanket they'd spread beneath a hundred-year-old tree.

Laurel sat cross-legged, looking comfortable and at ease. She slipped off her white strappy sandals.

"I don't have a picture of that."

He frowned, looking at the glass of wine he held. "You don't plan to be around five years from now?"

"I don't look that far ahead."

"You don't?" Scott had been looking ahead his entire life. "Why not?"

He glanced over at her and she turned away, hugging her knees up to her chest. "Growing up like I did, you learn not to look too far ahead, because what you see isn't what's going to be there when you reach that point."

A dull ache of compassion spread through him. "But what about now?" he asked. "You're in charge of your life now, not some faceless state employee."

"Am I?" Her gray eyes were almost bitter as she turned back to study him. "Can I tell the Fates to bring Paul back? Was I in charge when they took him in the first place?"

Scott pushed his food aside, no longer the least bit interested in it.

"It was an accident," he said softly, pleadingly. He was a pauper, begging for one small morsel of forgiveness.

"And how can I be in charge when 'accidents' happen around every corner?"

Sitting up, Scott gazed out into the surrounding meadow, searching for the peace he'd come there to find. He didn't know when he'd hated himself more than he did at that moment.

Not only was he responsible for his brother's death, he'd also killed Laurel's ability to hope.

"Don't you ever look forward to things?" he asked, not breathing as he waited for her answer.

She shook her head, eyes dry as she smiled sadly. "Not since Paul died. If good happens, I have plenty of time to enjoy it then. And the rest of the time, I'm not left with bitter disappointment when it doesn't."

"What about goals?" Scott just couldn't let this go. He needed her to have something left. An ability to believe. Have a little faith. Something. "You don't have a career as successful as yours without goals."

"Actually, you can," she said, her smile brightening just a bit, though her eyes were somber, remnants of the painful memories still resting there. "I didn't have any plans to be where I'm at at this stage. I thought I'd be married and raising children, not using my journalism degree."

"But after the accident, once you grew to be serious about a career, then you had goals." He watched her, wanting like hell to change things so that his time with her wasn't so short.

"Not really." She shook her head, her hair glinting pure gold in the rays of sunlight shining down through the leaves of the old maple. "I love what I do. But I got where I am by hard work, not planning. I didn't go after my current job. It was offered to me."

He picked a blade of grass and rolled it between thumb and forefinger.

"So how far ahead do you look?" he asked.

"A few months, maybe."

Scott thought that was one of the saddest things he'd ever heard—and knew he'd never climb out from beneath the weight of guilt.

"REMEMBER OUR SENIOR PROJECT?" Laurel asked Scott almost dreamily. Though the remains of their picnic still lay around them, they'd finished eating quite a while before, and were lounging quietly on the blanket, enjoying the peace of the late August afternoon. "What were there, fifty of us out here helping to tap the trees?"

Though she'd been desperately missing Paul, who was away at college that spring, the final semester of her senior year of high school had been one of the happiest times of her life.

"I remember we had to reschedule because a warm front blew in. We thought we'd never get started."

Maple trees could only be tapped when the nights were freezing and the days were mild. That was when the sap ran.

"We all had blisters on our hands from drilling those holes," she said, gazing toward the sugar bush and the scars of old holes in the trunks of the trees. "I remember worrying so much over whether or not I got the holes three inches deep. I didn't want to go too far and damage the tree—and if I didn't go far enough the sap wouldn't come out."

Scott wasn't looking at the trees. He was watching her, his eyes hooded. Laurel wished she knew what he was thinking.

She'd usually known what Scott was thinking. They'd spent a lot of time together that last semester of high school. Scott had appointed himself her protector in his brother's absence. And since Laurel's date was living a couple hundred miles away, Scott had stood in for Paul on several occasions.

"It's still hard to believe that a tree has to live forty years before it's ready to be tapped. And then it only gives ten gallons of sap a year."

"What'd Mr. Smith tell us? That for every ten gallons of sap he yielded only a quart of syrup?"

"Something like that."

She and her classmates had worked hard that spring, Scott included, to help the Smiths harvest their trees after Mr. Smith suffered a heart attack. Scott had driven her over almost every afternoon until the job was done.

He'd worked beside her drilling holes, hanging buckets, making her laugh. Making her forget how lonely she was, how much she was missing Paul.

Making her forget everything except that she was bonding with her classmates, being part of a family, a town.

Not only had they saved the Smiths financially that year, they'd helped Laurel discover happiness.

"YOU THINK YOU'LL EVER GET married?" Scott's question jarred Laurel from the hazy contentment she'd fallen into, throwing her back into a world she was quite happy to leave behind. She was lying flat on her back, staring up at the tree's branches. Scott was lying beside her, two feet of blanket, used paper plates and napkins between them. They each held a half-full cup of wine on their stomachs, occasionally raising their heads enough to take a sip.

She thought of Shane. Of how much she enjoyed his company, his wit.

Of how long he'd been waiting for them to be more than friends.

"I don't know."

"Do you want to?"

Did she? The question scared Laurel. "I guess. If I can be as sure as I was with Paul."

The sun was starting to go down. Laurel was sad to see that happen. She didn't want the day to end. She wanted to just continue lying there on that blanket with Scott close by and think about Paul. About belonging.

"Don't you want kids?"

She turned her head to look at him. "I used to." More than anything. A family of her own was the only thing Laurel could remember ever wanting.

"Used to?" His gaze was direct, searching.

Laurel's gaze returned to the leaves above. "I'm thirty-three," she said. "I'd have to do something relatively soon."

Back in New York Shane wanted children. And her.

But Laurel just wasn't sure.

"What about you?" she asked Scott. "I never pictured you growing old alone. Don't you want to get married?"

As she caught his gaze, his eyes seemed to be saying something to her. Laurel just couldn't figure out what. And then he looked away.

"Theoretically, yes."

Laurel chuckled. "What does that mean?"

"I have nothing against the institution of marriage, but, like you, it would have to be with the right person. Someone I not only wanted physically, but was best friends with as well."

Thoughts of him dating didn't bother her. Thoughts of him being best friends with someone Laurel didn't know did.

She guessed it was the protective-sister thing.

Except that, as she lay there next to Scott, she wasn't feeling sisterly at all.

"So you're saying you just haven't met the woman you want to marry yet," she said, refusing to pursue her own feelings any further.

She wasn't going to tarnish her friendship with Scott

by transferring her feelings for his brother onto him. He deserved far better than that.

"I've met her," Scott said, and Laurel's heart almost stopped.

"You have?"

She felt bereft. Someone else had Scott?

Why hadn't he said anything? Where was this woman while Laurel was lying here by Scott's side?

When he didn't answer, she looked over at him. He met her gaze only briefly, then nodded.

"So…"

"She isn't free."

"She's married?" Poor Scott.

"No."

"Does she return your feelings?"

This mattered a lot, and Laurel was really bothered by that fact.

"No."

She couldn't believe that, and ached for him. She also couldn't believe how relieved she felt.

"Has she said so?"

"No."

"Have you asked her?"

"No."

Laurel asked questions for a living. Ferreted out information for stories that would grab and hold the attention of millions of viewers. That was why she continued to question Scott.

She sensed a story.

"Does she know how you feel?"

"No."

Up on an elbow, she studied him. His eyes were closed, but she knew he was wide-awake. She could see his pulse throbbing. His thumb was tapping against the cup he held on the flat plane of his stomach.

"Then how do you know she doesn't return your feelings?"

His eyes opened and met hers. "I just do."

Laurel believed him.

She lay back again but couldn't find her earlier contentment. Knowing that Scott was in love left her feeling very unsettled.

The sun lowered slowly. There were still several hours of daylight left, but it was getting cooler.

"Do you ever wonder what's real and what's really just your head playing with you?" Laurel asked, breaking the long silence that had fallen between them.

"Not often," he said. "I just weigh the facts."

"But what if the facts, as you see them, aren't really the facts at all, but rather your head changing them to fit some preconceived picture you have?"

"But then that would still be reality, wouldn't it?" he asked. He was lying on his side, his head propped with his hand. He took a sip of wine. "Reality as you know it?"

"Twisting facts does not make them reality." She'd missed this so much—feeling comfortable enough with another person to just let her thoughts fly.

"Not if you knowingly twist them."

Lying on her stomach, resting up on her elbows, Laurel persisted. "But what if it's not knowingly, and so you act upon them, and then later find out that you had twisted them, after all."

He grimaced. "I think that happens to everyone at some point. Don't you?"

It wasn't the answer she'd been looking for. "I guess." She pondered some more. "So how do you protect yourself from making a mistake if there's no way to determine if you're making one? How do you keep your head from playing tricks on you?''

He was quiet for a moment. ''Maybe you don't.''

Laurel couldn't accept that. ''There's got to be some way to be able to trust yourself. I mean, if you can't even trust yourself, who can you trust?''

''You can trust yourself to do your best. It's all anyone *can* do. Their best.''

She shook her head. ''Not good enough.'' Not if it meant she was going to talk herself into marriage to Shane and then wake up one morning and find that she'd just been twisting loneliness into love, need into want.

Scott picked up a bottle of water, then rinsed their glasses and filled them. Settling back on his elbow he said, ''I guess being aware of the possibility goes a long way toward prevention.''

''Maybe.'' The fear remained.

''Talking it out with someone might be the best option,'' he said slowly, thoughtfully. ''If there's a hole in your logic, if your hypothesis is false, then someone who isn't traveling on the same mental journey would probably be able to detect the weak link.''

Laurel considered that a moment before asking, ''Do you think that, even after three and a half years, I could still be coping with Paul's loss by substituting someone else for him?''

His glance was suddenly completely focused. ''Do you think that's what you're doing?''

''No.''

He didn't say anything.

''I don't know,'' she said, changing her mind. ''I'm just so afraid to find out. Afraid to even try to replace him in case I'm just transferring my feelings for him to someone else.''

Only with Scott could she even be having this conversation, expressing fears she'd just started to admit to herself.

He'd seen her first thing in the morning, half-awake, with messy hair. He'd seen her sick with the flu.

He'd stood solid, taking her beating without flinching when he'd come to the church on her wedding day to tell her that Paul had been killed....

''You think he's the only man you can ever love?'' Scott asked.

Good question. ''I don't know, you know? I mean, I planned to love him for the rest of my life.''

''And now he's gone. And you still have a whole life ahead of you.''

''I know.''

She was watching a little black bug try to get over a wrinkle in the blanket. It would get almost to the top and then topple backward every time.

''So what if he was the only man I'll ever love,'' she said, expressing her thoughts as she had them. ''Is it wrong, then, to not want to be alone? To seek solace someplace?''

Scott took a sip of water. His blue eyes were intimate, probing as they held her gaze. ''I guess that depends on the situation. On the man. If you're honest with him, if he's not going to be hurt by the fact that you can't love him, then no, I don't think it's wrong.''

Laurel's heart lightened a little bit.

''As a matter of fact,'' he added, ''it's probably very right. People are here to offer other people solace. It's what we do. And as long as there's complete honesty...''

Yes, but...

"What if I don't know?" she whispered. "What if I think it could be love and then later find that it was just seeking solace? Then I've hurt him. And me, too."

She couldn't do it. She was going to be alone until she died. Or until, miraculously, she woke up one morning and found Paul nothing more than a fond memory.

"Life is full of risk, Laurel," Scott said. "Sometimes you just have to jump off the cliff and hope for the best."

"You really think so?"

"I do."

Laurel liked that. She liked him.

Enough to have the feeling be a huge source of confusion.

Scott was like a brother to her. He was her lover's brother. It had been that way for more than eighteen years.

Looking at him lying there, his body firm, strong—and so warm—she didn't want Scott to be her brother anymore.

She wanted those long fingers to leave that damn cup alone and touch her, pull her close to him. She wanted those arms around her, holding her.

It had been so long. Since that day in the churchyard when she'd finally quit hitting him and had fallen against him in shock, ready to sink to the ground and die if he hadn't wrapped his strong arms around her.

But today, she wanted more than support from Scott. More than comfort. She wanted passion. She wanted to taste those lips she'd known for more than half her life but never tasted.

She wanted him to taste her.

It was just her loneliness, the memories they shared and his resemblance to Paul that were making her feel this way. It was just that transference thing.

She knew that. Searching her heart, she knew with absolute doubt that she still loved Paul.

Lying here with Scott Hunter, she was not at the cliff. She could not jump.

CHAPTER NINE

HE WAS RUNNING OUT OF TIME. Scott had been watching the sun getting lower and lower in the sky, promising himself he'd tell her soon. In another few minutes. And then a few more. He just wanted to enjoy her company for as long as he could.

He was sitting up, forearms resting on his knees, while Laurel lay on her side, her head propped up on her hand. She finally looked relaxed.

He'd forgotten how great it was just to talk to Laurel. Had forgotten those long hours of conversation they used to have, the insights she'd given him, and the eager way her mind had absorbed ideas that were new to her.

Paul and their dad had always been close, whereas Scott had argued with the old man a lot. To their father, Paul was the perfect son, but Scott couldn't be like Paul, conservative, following such a narrow path. Scott had seen the world as a huge pool of opportunity, and needed to test all the waters. He'd known that without risk, there was no hope of greatness.

In high school, after Paul had left for college, Scott and his father had butted heads to the point where Scott had threatened to move out, and his dad hadn't tried to get him to stay.

Laurel had come over while he'd been packing his things. In her calm way she'd surveyed the situation, then turned her back and walked out of his room. He'd thought she'd left until he'd heard her quietly talking with his father.

And then she'd been back.

She'd helped him see that his dad viewed the world from an entirely different perspective than Scott did. She had helped him realize that in order to understand his father, he had to first look at his father's words and actions from his dad's perspective, not from his own. And with the awareness he'd gained by doing so, he found a way to help his father understand him.

Because of what Laurel had done for him, he'd unpacked and begun the first day of a new relationship with his father. A relationship that had never again faltered.

"Where are you?"

Her words were soft, bringing him back to the present.

Scott looked over at her. "Remembering how you saved my relationship with my dad."

"I didn't do anything. You were the one who was big enough to go to him. To open up your mind and listen to him."

"Only because you convinced me it was the right thing to do. And taught me how to listen to what he was saying."

"But you still had to be willing to swallow your pride and try. To ask him for another chance. You did the hard stuff, Scott. You always have."

No. He hadn't.

And it was time to tell her so.

"You have a strength beyond anything I've ever known," she continued.

He shook his head.

"You don't know how many times in the past three and a half years I've tapped into that strength. In my darkest times, just knowing you were out there, making the world a better place, gave me the jolt I needed to get up and do something—anything—that would help me rejoin the world.''

The man she was talking about was an illusion.

"I need you, friend," she said softly, her eyes wide and luminous. They were full of honesty and an openness that was rare in a girl who'd never been able to count on anything in her life.

Scott clenched his jaw and swallowed. He had to tell her. Didn't he?

If they spent any real time together, it would all come out eventually—the fact that he hadn't been driving the car because he'd been irresponsible and incapacitated. Paul had never been a good winter driver—Scott should have been at the wheel during that storm. And even if they'd had an accident, Scott would have been the one with the faulty seat belt, the one he'd had a recall notice for but just hadn't had time to take the car in for repair.

But what if they didn't spend time together? What if he was able to help her by leaving her illusions of him intact so she had something to cling to, to draw strength from?

What harm could that do?

As long as she had her life in New York, and he was here in Cooper's Corner...

As long as he didn't see her, didn't ever let her know that he was in love with her...

As long as he didn't do what he was longing to do— pull her beneath him and pour fifteen years' worth of love into her...

Glad as he was to have a reason not to confess his sins and face her anger and disrespect, Scott knew that this new plan was going to be the hardest of all to implement.

Because as he lay there with her, looking into her eyes,

he knew for certain that if he pulled her into his arms, she'd come willingly.

Life had found the cruelest way of all to make him pay....

"HOW QUICKLY CAN YOU BE READY?"

Showered and dressed, Laurel stood beside Maureen's desk on Wednesday morning to take the call. "Now."

"I'm on my way...."

Scott rang off before she could ask even a single question. He must know something.

He did. She could tell by the energy emanating from him as he met her out in the yard at Twin Oaks.

"Cecilia Hamilton was married to William Byrd's father for more than thirty-five years," he said without preamble. "He died three years ago."

Laurel wished she'd been sitting down. "What? How do you know? That doesn't even make sense." Her mind raced across the facts they'd accumulated. "Seth said Cecilia was in her late fifties."

"She's fifty-seven."

"William's three years older than that."

"I know."

"But..."

"She's from Boston and owns Hamilton Lending of New England, which has its corporate offices there. Guess who their biggest client is?"

"William?"

"No," Scott shook his head. "Renwick Construction."

She stared at him. "As in Leslie Renwick?" she asked slowly.

"Or her parents."

"Or maybe no relation at all?"

"Maybe. But that doesn't seem likely."

It took Laurel a couple of seconds to digest the impact of his news. "William's last name isn't Hamilton," was the only coherent thought she could come up with. "It's Byrd."

"A pen name."

Laurel looked up at him, impressed. "You have been busy."

"I just had a few more favors to call in. William's publisher called back, too. They haven't heard from him, but didn't expect to until next month."

Together they started to walk toward Twin Oaks. "So do we pay Hamilton Lending a visit?" Laurel asked, still trying to assimilate this new information.

"Not yet," Scott said, shaking his head. "Assuming Cecilia isn't missing, we have no business asking around without a warrant or alarming her employees. She could probably sue us for that."

"She was married to a man old enough to be her father," Laurel said. Her entire picture of the woman had changed in an instant.

"And then some. He was almost ninety when he died."

"It had to be for his money."

"That would be my guess."

Their hands brushed as they climbed the steps to the B and B. Embarrassed, Laurel jerked back.

"So where does William come to play in all this?"

"He's been in Connecticut for almost thirty years," Scott said. "My source told me he had nothing to do with his father after he left home."

They stopped on the porch outside the front door.

"Cecilia is the CEO and major stockholder of Hamilton Lending," he continued. "I'm guessing that either William was disowned—or he disowned them."

Frowning, Laurel felt some of the pieces fall into place.

."But now that William's father is dead, William isn't content to see his family fortune go to a gold digger, so he set up this meeting with Cecilia to do something about getting back his birthright."

"I was thinking along the same lines."

She wasn't surprised to find that, once again, she and Scott were on the same track. "So where does the Renwick birth certificate come in? Unless maybe Leslie was adopted. Is there a way to tell?"

"Not always, but yes, she was."

Laurel grinned at him. "Another favor?"

He nodded.

"There's more. According to the records of the hospital named on the birth certificate, there was a Cecilia Arnett listed as a patient that day."

"Leslie is Cecilia's? But that doesn't make sense. She was married. Why would she have a baby so far from home and give it away?"

He was standing so close she could feel his body heat. Touch him if she wanted to.

"How much you want to bet Cecilia had an affair or two along the way, found herself pregnant, went away to have the baby and gave it up for adoption?"

"William found out about the baby and is using the knowledge to blackmail Cecilia into giving him an interest in the company."

"Exactly."

She frowned and then continued. "But why are they *both* missing?"

"That's where I got stumped, too," Scott said, holding open the front door for her.

"So what do we do next?"

"Drive to Worcester, pay a visit to Leslie Renwick and see if she can shed any light on things."

"But what if she doesn't know Cecilia? What if she doesn't even know she's adopted? We can't just go barging in there...."

With a warm finger against her lips, Scott silenced her. "We won't let on to a thing," he assured her. "There are ways of asking questions without giving up any information."

Laurel's lips were still tingling from the touch of his finger when he closed the door behind them.

SCOTT HAD A SHORT MEETING with Maureen and Clint while Laurel was upstairs getting her things.

He filled them in on his progress with Cecilia Hamilton, giving, in deference to Maureen's former profession, more information than he usually did at this stage of a case, even one that was still unofficial. He told them that he and Laurel were going to make the three-hour drive to Worcester to pay Leslie Renwick a visit.

"Have you found any evidence of recent meetings between William and Cecilia?" Maureen asked, frowning. They were in the gathering room, standing by the registration desk, and she was tapping a pencil monotonously against the top of the computer.

Scott shook his head. "So far, it looks as though they just met for the first time in at least thirty years on Saturday at the café. There's nothing my sources have found so far. A single phone call a couple of weeks ago, but that appears to be all."

Clint reached over and gently removed the pencil from his sister's fingers. "News of Byrd's disappearance hit the New Ashford paper," he said. "We've already had one cancellation. Good news is it leaves a room open for Laurel."

Scott had just heard about the article that morning. Apparently it had run in yesterday's paper. The source appeared to be one of the guests who'd been staying at Twin Oaks the same time as Byrd. Though the police said there was no official investigation, no reason to suspect foul play, Scott still expected the story to be on the news all over this part of the state by evening.

Maureen's face was pinched, her ponytail not as neat as it had been the previous times Scott had met her. "I'm thinking of canceling this week's reservations," she said.

"I don't think that's necessary." Scott looked from one to the other.

"If either William or Cecilia was planning to blackmail the other, it doesn't make sense that they'd both disappear," Maureen said. "It seems more likely that something befell the two of them that had absolutely nothing to do with their reason for meeting. That something could be Carl Nevil."

"And if it is, we're responsible for whatever happened to William Byrd," Clint added. "We can't risk any more lives."

Scott stood, arms crossed, rubbing his lip with the back of his forefinger. "If Nevil is behind this, then he already has his victim. Maybe two of them."

Clint nodded.

Maureen looked from her brother to Scott. "If Nevil is behind this, any one of our guests could be next."

"She's right," Clint agreed, fingers in the front pockets of his slacks.

"I wouldn't cancel any reservations just yet," Scott said. "As soon as you do, you'll be confirming that there's a problem here and you stand to lose all your fall bookings."

"We aren't going to put our financial concerns above the welfare of innocent people," Clint protested.

"I don't think you will be," Scott told them. "If Owen and Carl Nevil are behind this, they aren't going to be stupid enough to do anything else right away. Not while everyone's watching the place so closely. Besides, there's no point. They haven't gotten the full benefit from their first hit yet. No need to waste another."

Maureen had to know that as well as he. She was probably just too spooked at the moment to be thinking objectively.

She was frowning. "How convinced are you that Owen's behind this?" she asked Scott. "On a scale of one to ten."

"Two, maybe three, but only because he's not available for questioning."

She nodded. "Then I guess we just sit and wait."

Scott was going to do everything he could to make that excruciating period of waiting as short as possible for her.

THE DRIVE ACROSS THE STATE of Massachusetts was a beautiful one. The first hints of gold and red appeared in the dark green canopy of trees that shaded the highway, and the brilliant colors of the distant meadows had deepened, sure signs of the approaching fall.

For the first part of the drive, Laurel and Scott reviewed the evidence they had so far, this time with Laurel's tape recorder running. They ended up right where they'd been the day before—desperately needing to know more.

If William and Cecilia's disappearance had nothing to do with their reason for meeting, then where were they? Could it be that someone was after one of them and got two in the bargain? And why had the Renwicks' names been whited out on that birth certificate?

When Scott's cell phone rang about half an hour after

they'd left Cooper's Corner, Laurel hoped for good news, until she saw the disappointment cross Scott's face.

"The fingerprints lifted from Byrd's room were inconclusive," he said, ending the call.

"If we're working with a professional, they would be," Laurel said, voicing what they both already knew.

"There also just might not have been any clear prints because there weren't any clear prints."

She supposed, but too many things were adding up to keep pointing to simple happenstance.

"You know, rather than a random crime, someone could easily be after Cecilia. She's worth a bundle."

"Which explains the security level at her house," Scott added.

"The guy could have been waiting at her house for her to arrive."

"Though I hope you're wrong, the explanation fits."

She'd been hoping Scott would find a hole in her logic. Watching as the Massachusetts landscape whizzed past her window, Laurel tried to find the optimism she'd held on to for the past couple of days. But her heart filled with dread as she thought of the older man, now missing for four days. If something bad had happened to him, if he'd suffered…

"What reason are we going to give Ms. Renwick for showing up at her home?" Laurel asked, needing a different track for her thoughts.

She'd done some laundry at Twin Oaks and was wearing her white slacks again with her favorite black short-sleeved sweater, but wished she'd chosen something else. The day was turning out to be very hot.

Scott shrugged, one hand on the wheel, the other resting along the window beside him. "I don't know for sure, yet," he said. "But I won't lie to her. I can't tell her the whole truth, of course, but I'm always honest."

Laurel knew that about him—the newspaper article he'd had published without her permission notwithstanding. She remembered the time he'd sideswiped his dad's car pulling out of a fast-food drive-through. The elder Hunter had assumed that someone had dinged the car in a parking lot, leaving Scott off the hook.

He'd confessed, anyway, and had to submit to an entire Saturday afternoon of driving through pylons with his father in the parking lot of Theodore Cooper Elementary School.

"Does that mean we tell her you're a cop?" Laurel asked, hating to worry the woman when they didn't really know for sure yet that there was anything to worry about.

She was relieved when Scott shook his head. "Until this case becomes official, we'll leave my profession out."

"Can we tell her that we found her birth certificate in the room of a bed-and-breakfast in Cooper's Corner and wanted to return it to her?"

He grinned at her. "You're better at this than you let on. That would be a great place to start. We can use that to lead into asking her if she has any idea why it might have been there."

"And what do we do if she asks whose room we found it in?"

"We tell her that no one was in the room at the time."

"Which is technically true, but…"

"In this case, 'technically' is going to have to do."

"And what do we do if she pushes for more information?"

His jaw tense, Scott stared straight ahead. "Assuming we've ascertained that she knows she's adopted, we tell her as much of the truth as we know. It's her birth certificate we're holding. She probably has the right to know.''

When he put it like that, Laurel couldn't argue. She just would rather not be the bearer of bad news. She knew how horrible it felt to be the receiver.

Watching Scott's hand on the steering wheel, Laurel was struck with how absolutely horrible it must have been for him to be the one to tell her about Paul's death.

At the time she'd only been able to think about the fact that Paul was gone, and it had taken her a long time to comprehend that.

But Scott had suffered a loss, too. His brother was dead, and before he could grieve, he had to break the news to Laurel.

He'd told her with such gentleness, such love and compassion. She wondered where, in the midst of his own pain, he'd found so much strength to give to her.

Gratitude filled her heart to overflowing. Gratitude and love for this man who'd been such a good brother to her— better, she was sure, than if she'd had the biological sibling she'd always longed for.

Sometime before she went back to New York, she was going to thank him for that.

''TELL ME SOMETHING,'' Scott said now, his brow clear as he relaxed back, one hand on the wheel, the other casually thrown across the armrest between them. ''How is it that you can always figure out the right way in to other people's thought processes?''

She turned off her tape recorder.

''I've spent my life fitting into other people's lives.'' Survival in the foster system meant having to quickly ascertain, in every new environment, just what the family needed. Why they were opening their home to her. Her only hope of being able to stay awhile was to answer that need.

"That sounds painful."

"Not really." Laurel slipped out of her sandals and put one foot up on the corner of the dash. "When you make those around you feel good, you're generally making yourself feel good, too."

"Is that what you did with Paul?"

"No," Laurel sighed. "He was the exception."

Scott didn't say anything so she continued. "Paul was the first person I can remember who tried to please me before I even thought about trying to please him. When we were together, he was always concerned about my comfort, both physically and otherwise."

"You were always doing things for him, too."

"Of course. I loved him."

"I looked out for you."

Her heart rate sped up at the intimate tone, and to her dismay, her stomach churned with desire.

"I know you did," she said softly. And then, out of self-preservation, she reminded both of them, "Your dad did, too. You guys were a first for me."

"But there've been others since?"

Laurel thought about that. "No," she finally said. "There's been no one since."

SCOTT HADN'T MEANT the conversation to turn so serious. After the night before, he'd been determined to do exactly the opposite. But he just couldn't leave well enough alone.

"What about you? And your needs?" he challenged. "Don't you sometimes just need things for yourself?"

"I only need to be able to do what I can to make the

people around me happy so they'll keep me around." A smile accompanied the words. She was joking.

But Scott knew there was truth in those words.

Frustration welled up inside him. He loved her. He could give her the security she'd always craved. The sense of belonging.

And yet he knew it was the one thing he'd never have the opportunity to do.

AS THEY CROSSED THE STATE, the landscape—and the road signs—began to change. Orchards gave way to bogs. Advertisements for sugar bush tours and roadside stands selling maple syrup gave way to signs for cranberry-harvesting tours, a cranberry museum and the Massachusetts Cranberry Harvest Festival.

The bogs were impressive, stretching as they did for acres and acres.

"Did you know that for every acre of cranberry bog, growers have an additional four acres of supporting land?" Scott asked.

She frowned, looking out at the bog they were passing. A sprinkler system was completely soaking the land, except where workers appeared to be pulling weeds. She'd been living on this side of the state for several years, Laurel thought, yet she knew practically nothing about the cranberry industry.

"Supporting land?" she asked.

"Wetlands, uplands, ditches, flumes, ponds—sources for the fresh water supply the plants require…"

Scott continued, rattling off statistics like an audio encyclopedia. Facts about the berries, the growers, the economics.

Laurel absorbed the information, fascinated by how much Scott knew. He'd often regaled them with a wealth of nonessential facts. Paul and his father had humored him, but Laurel, feeling like a little kid, had soaked it all up.

"Because pollination is essential to a cranberry crop, growers use an average of one to two beehives per acre of bog," he added.

Laurel looked out the window for the hives, knowing that Paul would have teased her for doing so.

It wasn't that Paul had been mean—or even small-minded. He'd just enjoyed teasing her about her voracious need to know everything. But he'd also told her he'd loved her unending curiosity.

Paul was extremely intelligent. His IQ was probably genius level if anyone had cared to find out. But his knowledge was as focused as his life had been. He knew everything about the things that affected him and little about anything that he couldn't use directly.

Scott, on the other hand, knew all kinds of interesting facts that had no practical application other than broadening the mind and fostering an appreciation of life and the larger world around him.

The bog stretched as far as she could see.

"I wonder how they harvest all that."

Scott shifted, stretching one long leg. "A couple of different ways, depending on what they're going to use the cranberries for."

"You going to tell me what they are?" she asked, with a nudge to his arm when he left her hanging there.

It felt good touching him.

It also felt good to listen as he told her about the harvesting methods and the wildlife in the bogs as well.

"Is there anything you don't know?" Laurel asked, chuckling.

Scott glanced over at her, his gaze holding hers for a

heady second. Then his grin faded. "Plenty," he said, turning his attention back to the road.

Laurel wondered what had brought about the sudden change of mood.

But that was one question she didn't feel free to ask.

CHAPTER TEN

THE NEIGHBORHOOD WAS NEW. Middle class. The homes were based on three or four models, and the yards were large enough to play tag on, freshly mown and green. Leslie lived about halfway down the block in a cozy bungalow with black shutters and a white picket fence. The house was rimmed with flower beds blooming with riotous color.

Crossing her fingers as Scott pulled up in front of the house, Laurel opened her door.

"Doesn't look like anyone's home," Scott said.

She didn't want to think that. "Her car's probably in the garage. And you don't need lights this early in the day."

Of course, the morning papers still on the mat by the front door were a little harder to ignore.

Scott picked them up. "The last few days' are here."

His eyes met Laurel's above the stack in his arms and her blood ran cold.

"You think we're going to find out that she's missing, too, don't you?"

"I'm not saying that."

"But you're thinking it."

The papers in his arms said what he wouldn't. They'd found a similar pile at Cecilia's house. He knocked, anyway.

And then knocked a second time.

"Leslie could just be gone on vacation," he said after the third knock.

"Then why didn't she cancel the newspaper? Isn't that what people normally do when they go out of town? Or at least ask a neighbor to pick them up?"

"Usually, but not everyone's that organized."

Laurel nodded, though she wasn't buying a word of it. She suspected he was only saying those things for her benefit, trying to leave her a little bit of the optimism she'd started with four days before. But while she appreciated the effort, she knew the situation didn't look good.

She was almost afraid to continue. Was every clue going to lead to another missing person? Where would it end?

"Let's take a look around," Scott said, heading back down the steps and around the side of the house. He searched under every window for footprints and checked for any sign of forced entry. Laurel chose to be encouraged when he found nothing.

And then Scott walked over to the garage and peered in the window.

"I'll be damned," he said.

Heart in her throat, Laurel stood up on her toes to see what he'd found.

There, parked by itself in the middle of a two-car garage, was Cecilia's Crown Victoria.

IT DIDN'T LOOK GOOD. Spinning through the facts in his mind, Scott tried to find a positive explanation for the seemingly unplanned disappearances of every key player he came across in this case that wasn't a case. And found none. Something bad was afoot, he was certain of it.

"Maybe they all decided to visit Leslie's adopted parents and took her car instead of Cecilia's," Laurel said as she walked briskly beside him down the sidewalk to the neighbor's front door.

She was trying to find that happy ending, too. "The Renwicks are dead. Have been for several years."

"Oh."

They walked silently for a couple of steps, then Laurel asked, "Do you think Leslie could be the culprit, somehow? Or is she another victim?"

He'd been wondering the same thing. "My hunch is she's a victim—a culprit probably wouldn't leave the victim's car in her garage—but I'm keeping my mind open to any possibility."

They found a total of three people home on Leslie's block. The third of the three, a woman about their age who lived directly across the street, seemed to know Leslie the best.

"We do dinner and a movie at least once a week," the woman told them when they asked if she knew Leslie. "It's my date night out away from the kids," she added. "I'm a stay-at-home mom with two little ones still in diapers, and my husband makes certain he's home early at least one night a week to watch them for me so I can play with the big kids."

The pretty blond woman smiled, and Scott noticed how naturally Laurel smiled back. It amazed him how she seemed able to sympathize with anyone in any situation.

Laurel looked beyond the woman to the quiet house behind her. "Do you need to check on your kids?" she asked.

"They're both asleep," the woman said. "I'm Katy Miller, by the way. So what's up with Leslie? You two friends of hers?"

"Not exactly." Scott took his notebook out of his

pocket. His badge was attached. "I'm with the Massachusetts State Police, though I'm here unofficially."

Katy's easy demeanor changed instantly to one of concern. "Did something happen to Leslie?" she asked, clutching the front door with both hands as if bracing for bad news.

"We aren't certain," Scott told her. "We hope not. We just wanted to ask you a few questions, hoping you'd be able to help clear things up for us."

"Is she in some kind of trouble?" Katy's face was shuttered.

"Again, we hope not," Scott sighed. "I need to reiterate that I'm not here in any official capacity. My superiors know that I'm working on this case, but I'm doing it as a favor to a friend."

Katy seemed to sink even lower, and Scott was suddenly more glad than ever to have Laurel there with him. She'd know what to do if the woman became emotional. "Leslie's missing?" Katy whispered.

"Maybe," Scott said. "When was the last time you saw her?"

"Late Saturday afternoon. She was over here for lunch but left before we started the movie we'd rented."

"Did you find that odd?"

"No," Katy said, shaking her head. "She's a workaholic and heads home early a lot."

As quickly and succinctly as he could, Scott filled Katy in on the bits of the case he felt free to tell her, ending with the fact that Cecilia's car was in Leslie's garage and there were several days' worth of papers on Leslie's doorstep. He didn't, however, mention that Leslie was adopted or that they suspected Cecilia was her birth mother.

"So, at this point, we're just looking for any clues that might tell us where she's gone," he concluded. "Does she live alone? Can you tell us anything about her friends? Where she works?''

Katy was willing to tell them whatever she could to help them find her friend. She said Leslie lived alone, and had for the five years she'd been here.

"What does she do for a living?" Laurel asked softly, her expression warm. Scott could see why she was so good at her job. One of those looks directed at him and he'd have told her anything she wanted to know.

"She's a writer," Leslie said, looking from one to the other. "She does freelance technical writing for people all over the United States."

"So she works at home?"

Katy nodded. "She comes over here for lunch sometimes to give us both a chance at conversation."

Leslie had a lot of friends, she told them, though only two really close ones—Katy and a woman Leslie had known since grade school. That woman now lived in Ohio.

"Do you think Leslie would have gone there if she was on the run from something?" Scott asked.

"Maybe." Katy leaned her head against the door. "Except that she and her husband are in Europe for a month."

Jotting everything down, Scott stopped for a moment, sheer frustration preventing him from carrying on with his questioning.

There had to be something he was missing. A clue that was staring him in the face...

"She does have a new boyfriend, though," Katy added, almost as an afterthought.

Or a player he wasn't aware of.

Scott looked up. "How new?"

"I don't know. A month, maybe." Katy straightened, though she didn't loosen her grip on the door.

Laurel gave her a gentle smile. "Have you met him?"

Katy's expression turned pensive as she shook her head. "Leslie doesn't talk much about him. I don't even know his name. I've just seen him coming and going a couple of times. I suspected she was keeping quiet about him because he's so much older than her."

"Older?" Scott and Laurel exchanged a glance. "How much older?"

"I don't know, since I didn't actually meet him." Katy looked worried as her glance swept from one of them to the other. "Ten, fifteen years, maybe."

"Can you tell us what he looked like?" At that moment, Scott felt like hugging the pretty housewife. Finally, a real clue.

"Tall, a classic California beachboy type except older. There was definite gray in his dark hair. He was really handsome, though."

"Do you remember what kind of car he drove?"

"No." Katy frowned. "He never seemed to drive. He was in Leslie's car the times I saw him."

That fact was awarded its own page in Scott's little notebook.

Though he and Laurel visited with Katy for another ten minutes, they didn't learn anything else that was useful. But they'd gained an ally. If Katy noticed anyone anywhere near Leslie's house, she was going to call Scott's cell phone immediately.

Along with everyone else he'd talked to in the last couple of days.

Scott just hoped the damn thing would start ringing.

"YOU WANT TO HEAD BACK to Cooper's Corner?" he asked as they returned to the Blazer, buckling their seat belts.

"There doesn't seem to be much point in hanging around here." She and Scott were both frustrated and tired.

And spending far too much time together for Laurel's peace of mind.

Within moments, they had a plan. They'd return to Cooper's Corner. Scott was going to visit a few people and see how many more favors he could cash in on. He wanted to find out more about both Cecilia and William, like what kind of purchases they'd made recently on their credit cards. That sort of thing.

Laurel thought she'd spend a little more time downtown. Maybe there was someone who had overheard the couple talking during their time at the diner Saturday afternoon.

"Didn't you have plans for this vacation of yours?" she asked Scott after several minutes of silent driving.

He looked at her for a long moment. "No."

"But it's your free time," Laurel said, frowning, slipping her feet out of her sandals. "Surely you had something in mind."

He didn't say anything, just pulled into the fast lane to pass a semi.

With both feet up on the dash, Laurel ran her hands along the white slacks that had been ironed and crisp that morning. "What *do* you do in your free time?" she asked. Scott had said so little about his life. The only thing she really knew was that the woman he loved didn't return his feelings—didn't even know about them.

That was still gnawing at her.

"I don't have a lot of free time."

"You have to have days off."

He shrugged.

"You still ski every chance you get?"

"Not really."

"When was the last time you went up?"

"I don't remember."

Frowning, Laurel got a queer feeling in her stomach. "Approximately."

"A year or two, maybe more."

"How many times have you been up since Paul died?"

"I don't know." He shifted in his seat and glanced over at her. "Maybe none."

Something was wrong.

"More like, for sure none," she said.

"Maybe."

"What about your bike?" she asked. "You still riding in marathons?"

"Not lately."

"When was the last time you did that?"

"I don't know," Scott said, his voice edgy. "Why the inquisition all of a sudden?"

"I don't know." She deliberately repeated what he'd been telling her. "What about skydiving? You been up anytime in the last three years?"

"Not that I can remember."

"How about climbing? Canoeing? Camping?"

"No." His jaw tight, he slouched back, one hand on the wheel, as though trying to appear relaxed.

"Scott?"

"Yeah?"

She waited until he glanced over at her. "Do you do anything you love to do anymore?"

"I love my job."

She believed that. "But work isn't enough."

"It is for me."

"There's more to life than work!" That had been a

hard lesson for her to learn, but she'd mastered it almost two years ago.

He didn't answer her.

What was going on here?

"So you're telling me that when Paul died you gave up every interest you'd ever had?"

"Maybe."

"Why?"

"I guess I didn't notice."

"Bullshit."

He shot her a sharp glance. "I'm not the first man to bury myself in work and get comfortable there."

Probably not. So why did she have a very strong feeling that there was more to his withdrawal than a man forgetting to come up for air?

"I'm a detective now, Laurel." He spoke with confidence. "More times than not, I'm helping to save lives. It's hard not to let that take priority."

She studied him, wishing she could see inside his mind—or better, his heart. "You're sure that's all it is?"

"I'm sure."

She might have let him convince her—if he'd only looked her in the eye when he'd lied to her.

THEY STOPPED ONCE FOR GAS, about halfway between Worcester and Cooper's Corner. As much as she needed some time away from Scott, time to collect her thoughts, to remember who she was, and who she wasn't, Laurel was sad that their trip was almost at an end. After several days in Scott's company, she wasn't looking forward to going their separate ways that afternoon.

And because of that, she couldn't get away from him fast enough.

Scott's cell phone rang just as they were pulling back

onto the highway. As she listened to the one-sided conversation, Laurel's adrenaline pumped quickly, making it hard for her to sit still. She couldn't wait for him to hang up and explain his hard-hitting "How much?" followed by "You're sure?"

"More than a million dollars has been transferred from Cecilia's accounts," he said as soon as she clicked off the phone. "An electronic transfer first thing Sunday morning."

He changed lanes, allowing a speeding Mustang to pass them.

"That's three days ago."

"The day after she and William first went missing."

"He was blackmailing her, then."

"It looks that way."

Laurel was surprised at the depth of the disappointment that shot through her. She'd really been hoping that they'd been wrong about the older gentleman.

"Did she turn it into cash?"

Scott shook his head. "It was a straight transfer, but I don't know where it was transferred to. My source wouldn't give me that much. He could lose his job for telling me as much as he did."

Laurel nodded, though she wished Scott had pushed a little harder. They really needed a break soon or she feared their chances of finding the women alive were going to be slim.

"So." She frowned, turning sideways in her seat so she could watch him. "If that's the case, and William got his money, why were they visiting Leslie? And what happened to them?"

"Maybe only Cecilia came here."

"Then where's William? Why wouldn't he have returned to Twin Oaks for his stuff?"

Scott was silent for a moment. Laurel loved the intensity she read on his features as he worked over the facts. "He's probably still with Cecilia," he finally said. "And Leslie. And beyond that, I haven't got any ideas, except that something in somebody's plan went horribly wrong."

"Or horribly right."

At the next exit he slowed, took the ramp, and then rejoined the highway heading in the opposite direction.

"So where are we going now?"

"Cecilia's office."

"In Boston?"

His look was direct. "You have any better idea?"

"None."

"We might not make it back to Twin Oaks tonight."

"I'm okay with that."

She needed to find Byrd as badly as he did. To know that the old man, blackmailer or not, was really okay. To know that her trip to Cooper's Corner was not a failure. To get her story.

To be able to get back to the life she lived in New York. A life where she was successful. Content. Verging on happy. And alone.

HAMILTON LENDING OF New England had impressive offices housed in a smoke-windowed high-rise in the middle of downtown Boston. A glass-encased directory inside the marbled lobby told them that Hamilton's executive offices were on the eighteenth floor.

"Nothing like living on the top," Laurel said dryly as she followed Scott into the elevator.

He just hoped they made it to the top with few stops. Being alone with Laurel in that enclosed space had him thinking things he couldn't afford to think. The emergency button was only a couple of inches away. He could stop the elevator, stop time and pretend that the world consisted of only the two of them.

Of course, then the elevator would start again.

Cecilia's administrative assistant was in her office. Bettina Warren was in her early forties, with short dark hair and stern features. Dressed in no-nonsense business attire, the woman could have been a sergeant in the army.

And she guarded her army—Cecilia—very zealously.

"Do you have a warrant to be here?"

Her first question didn't bode well for the remainder of the visit. Or for the hope that they would gain a thing from being there. Scott glanced at Laurel, and with a lowering of his lids, he turned the next few minutes over to her.

"The thing is," she said, sitting on the edge of one of the hard wooden chairs in front of Ms. Warren's desk, "this is not an official investigation at all. We started out doing a favor for a friend and have grown increasingly concerned about the welfare of two other people we've never met. One of them is Cecilia Hamilton. At this point we'd like only for you to hear us out. If, after that, you want us to leave, we'll do so immediately without speaking to another person in the company."

If Scott hadn't been so besotted with Laurel, he'd have had to interrupt her already. He couldn't make that promise.

But she had. And he was damn well going to have to abide by it. Melting into the back of the room, he comforted himself with the sure knowledge that Laurel was going to win Ms. Warren's trust—which would make keeping that promise a moot point.

She went on to give Cecilia's assistant more information than Scott would have. She didn't, of course, mention anything that was, at that moment, only theory, like William's possible blackmail scheme or the fact that Cecilia might very well be Leslie Renwick's birth mother.

She looked so beautiful sitting there, her features animated with the empathy and apprehension she was feeling. She literally took his breath away—and for a second, rational thought, as well, as he tried to imagine an entire lifetime without her.

When Laurel fell quiet, the drill sergeant leaned forward, hands resting a body's width apart on her desk. "What do you need to know?" she asked Laurel.

It wasn't often that Scott found himself invisible, but on some level, the experience was not altogether a bad one.

"When was the last time you saw or heard from Cecilia?" Laurel asked.

"She was up here last week, finishing up business so that she could spend the rest of the summer in New Ashford."

"When did she leave here?"

"Saturday morning. She was meeting someone in Cooper's Corner before going out to her place."

"Do you know who she was meeting?"

"No, though I suspected it might be a man."

Laurel's back was straight, her body still as she perched on the edge of the chair, facing Ms. Warren. Scott had the distinct feeling she was aware of him behind her, though.

"Does she date often?" Laurel asked the question Scott would have.

"No. Not at all. Which is why I think she was seeing a man. She was completely evasive—and a little nervous and shy—about the meeting. I've been here for twenty years and I've never seen Ms. Hamilton act that way."

Wishing he felt comfortable enough to take out his

notebook, Scott settled for inscribing that last telling remark in caps on his mental notepad.

"And you haven't heard from her since the meeting?"

"No."

"Is that unusual?"

"Very," Ms. Warren said, her right thumb tapping on a file. She might be the epitome of control, but the woman was worried.

And that worried Scott.

"But then so is buying a summer home three hours from the company. I've just been telling myself this is all part of the recovery-from-grief process. Though Mr. Hamilton was so old, Ms. Hamilton is still a relatively young woman with a lot of years ahead of her."

As Scott silently surveyed the room, compiling a character sketch of Cecilia Hamilton, the two women chatted about the indomitable businesswoman Cecilia had become over the years. And the loyal, compassionate and caring employer as well.

Scott added everything to his checklist. "Did she have any family other than Mr. Hamilton's son, William?" he asked when Laurel reached the end of her questioning.

"The only family I've ever known of is a younger brother," she said, meeting Scott's gaze directly.

Coming forward, he took the seat next to Laurel, giving her a quick glance of gratitude and praise.

"Does he work here?" he asked the older woman.

Bettina Warren shook her head. "He's in prison—has been for the past ten years."

Scott's internal alarm started to peal. "What's he up for?"

"Hustling and drugs, mostly, but from what I understand, he's been in trouble on and off since he was a teenager."

"Cecilia talks to you about this?" Laurel's gaze was intent on the other woman. Scott could almost see the human-interest story churning inside her mind.

"Never," Ms. Warren surprised Scott by saying. "Ms. Hamilton was like a mother hen with that man, always sticking up for him, protecting him. But in an office like this you hear things, you know?"

Ms. Warren glanced toward the two doors across from her. They both had nameplates. One for Ms. Hamilton and one for her late husband. It didn't take a detective to figure out that Cecilia's assistant had overheard a conversation or two between husband and wife.

"Dennis Arnett was the only thing I ever heard the two of them fight about—maybe because her brother was the only reason she ever stood up to him. Mr. Hamilton was a pretty stern man. People didn't cross him often."

With only one more piece of helpful information forthcoming—the name of the prison Dennis Arnett, Cecilia's fifty-four-year old brother, was in—Laurel and Scott prepared to take their leave. They made sure Bettina Warren had Scott's cell phone number—and obtained her assurance that she'd call the second she thought of anything else.

NOT FOR THE FIRST TIME, Laurel desperately wished that Scott were Paul as she sat with him at a diner across the street from Hamilton Lending and watched him make a series of calls, trying to find out what he could about Dennis Arnett.

Immediately she felt guilty for being disloyal to Scott, her very dear friend. She should be celebrating her chance to be with him again. And then, in her twisted way, she felt guilty for the disloyalty to Paul that thought generated.

It hadn't quite been dinnertime when they'd left Bettina

Warren, so they'd just ordered coffee. Black. Laurel was seriously considering loading up with enough cream to dilute the thick liquid, but wasn't sure how to get enough room in her cup to do so.

Drinking the nasty stuff to make room was not an option.

She noticed that after an initial sip, Scott hadn't touched his cup, either.

She'd already given her impressions of the afternoon to the trusty little machine in her purse and was eager for Scott to get off the phone and tell her what he'd found out about Dennis Arnett.

"He's out of prison." Scott's voice was clipped as he dropped his cell phone on the table. "He got out last month. Has a place in Worcester…"

Heart pounding, Laurel held his gaze, trying to read his mind. "Where Leslie's from."

His nod couldn't have been more serious.

"You think he's involved in all of this?"

"I think we'd be remiss to dismiss the possibility."

"What would he be after?" Rearranging her silverware on the paper napkin on which it lay, Laurel came up with her own silent answers to her question.

"Money would be the obvious thing. He has a very wealthy sister."

That had been her guess.

"But from what Ms. Warren said, that Cecilia was always protecting him, wouldn't you think she'd just give it to him?"

"Unless his years in prison made him greedy and he asked for more than she was willing to part with. You have to consider this was a woman who gave up her youth to marry a sugar daddy. Money's got to be pretty big on her list of priorities."

She frowned, only now realizing something that had been bothering her. "Ms. Warren's description of Cecilia sure doesn't fit the profile of a gold digger, does it?"

Shaking his head, Scott added several packs of sugar to his coffee. "People change. Plus, you have to consider that Bettina Warren is Cecilia's employee. She's bound to have a biased view."

"It's also possible that Cecilia wasn't a gold digger at all. Maybe she just fell in love with William Sr. and wanted to spend her life with him."

"Anything's possible." Scott didn't sound as if he thought it likely, though, and that bothered Laurel a lot.

"So where do we go from here?" she asked.

"I put a call into his parole officer, but he'd already left for the day. I think he's our next bet."

Without even tasting the coffee to see if there was any improvement, Scott threw a couple of bills on the table and stood.

"Shall we go?"

Laurel followed him as naturally and willingly as if she'd vowed to do so for the rest of her life.

She almost stalled in her tracks. Where had that thought come from?

She'd just confused him with Paul again. That had to be it. It wouldn't happen again.

HE'D NEVER KNOWN TORTURE could be so sweet. All day as they'd driven across the state, and now again, encased in the close confines of the Blazer with Laurel, her lilac scent filling the air, Scott could have been in heaven.

If he hadn't already earned his entrance to hell.

Hour after hour he'd talked to her, listened to her laugh at the jokes he told, heard about some of the more heart-wrenching stories she'd covered. Hour after hour he'd imagined what it would have been like if he'd been the one she'd fallen in love with all those years ago.

It was a dangerous road to travel.

As an officer of the law, Scott knew better than to court danger. He had enough of it come his way all by itself.

"I'd like to head back toward Worcester," Scott said, "so we can meet with Arnett's parole officer first thing in the morning."

He held his breath, waiting for Laurel to agree. Hoping that she would—and that she wouldn't.

She did.

It was hard to believe, as they arrived back in Worcester, that they'd been there only that morning. Even for Scott, it had been one hell of a long day. He got them a couple of rooms in a well-known roadside motel. Generic, but nice enough to have thick towels and a basket full of free toiletries in the bathroom. Most important, it was clean.

"You hungry?" Laurel asked as they stood outside the doors to their adjoining rooms. They'd had a late lunch, but that had been hours ago.

"A little," Scott said. He'd been thinking of room service.

"You want to order a pizza and watch a movie?"

If it hadn't been for the flash of vulnerability he'd seen in her eyes, he'd have said no immediately. He'd already told himself—unequivocally—that he was going to leave her at her door and not see or speak to her again until he picked her up in the morning.

"Sure." He cursed himself for the fool he knew himself to be.

He wasn't made of iron.

SHE STILL PICKED THE CHEESE off her pizza, eating it first, and saving the crust until last. It had always driven him crazy.

So did the way she licked her fingers, her tongue savoring every one, as though the appendage were part of the meal itself. He'd been ashamed more than once to find himself fantasizing about his tongue tasting her that way. And other ways as well...

"You think William's dead?" she asked, frowning down at a piece of half-burnt pepperoni.

"No." He wasn't ready to believe that.

"You think William and Cecilia got to Leslie's and then Dennis came and surprised them all?"

"Or maybe Leslie and Dennis surprised them. Let's not forget, the Renwicks are Hamilton's biggest client. As Cecilia's brother, it's not completely impossible that Dennis would have known Leslie. Maybe she fell in love with him, which he could have used to his advantage. They might be working together."

"Do you really think that would have happened? That Cecilia would have let her brother be around her own daughter?"

"No."

"Me, neither."

"I'm not ready to rule out the possibility that Dennis knows Leslie now, however," he said, pushing the box of pizza away. He'd had enough. "Or that someone is willing to do something life threatening to get their hands on the money Cecilia transferred."

"William's been gone five days without even so much as calling Twin Oaks to say he's been delayed. Foul play's a strong possibility."

Scott was pretty much certain that Byrd was not missing of his own accord. "I'm not giving up hope that we'll find him unharmed," he said.

And he wasn't.

But as each day passed, hope was waning.

SHE'D RENTED *While You Were Sleeping,* from the in-room movie selection. A romantic comedy about a woman pretending to be the fiancée of a man who is comatose in the hospital after an accident, the movie seemed an innocuous choice. Though it was a few years old, neither of them had seen it before.

Unless it was on late-night television, Scott hadn't seen a movie in three and a half years, and was thankful Laurel didn't ask why not.

He was glad she'd chosen a comedy. As far as he was concerned they'd had enough drama that week.

Lying back on one bed, she'd waited for him to settle on the other before starting the movie. If he turned himself just a little and propped his head up on both pillows, he could almost not see her lying on the bed next to him. It wasn't as if this was the first time they'd been in a motel room together. There'd been several times when he had taken trips with Laurel and Paul for one reason or another. She and Paul had shared one bed, while he'd lain awake all night in the other, burning up with need—and jealousy of the older brother he'd adored.

The movie was cute, the heroine funny and compelling as she made her way through life alone, creating her own happiness where there was no one else to create it for her.

In many ways, she reminded him of Laurel.

No matter what life handed to Lucy in the movie, she wasn't hard or bitter. Even losing her beloved father did not strip her of her belief in good things to come.

Lying there, more emotionally than physically exhausted, Scott thought of how alone Laurel was in the

world. Yet like the movie heroine she didn't let that aloneness harden her heart or sour her on life.

He found himself falling in love with Laurel all over
again.

They were about halfway through the movie before he
realized she was crying. Quietly the tears rolled down her
cheeks. He didn't know when she'd availed herself of a
tissue, but ·as he watched, she surreptitiously wiped her
nose without making a sound.

She was trying so hard to cover her reaction to the
movie that he wondered if maybe it would be kinder to
pretend he didn't notice. Damn that movie for billing itself
as a comedy when it was causing Laurel such grief.

With a furtive glance in his direction, Laurel caught
him watching her—not the movie. He knew he should
look away. His conscience told him he *had* to look away.
Danger lurked in the emotion-laden air between them.

But those beautiful gray eyes were filled with heartache
and loneliness, and he couldn't look away.

CHAPTER ELEVEN

"YOU WANT TO TALK ABOUT IT?"

Laurel shook her head.

She did want to. So badly. She just didn't know how. Having spent so much of her life hurting inside by herself, she hardly knew what else to do.

"You sure?" Scott's gaze was soft, inviting.

She nodded, but she couldn't quit crying. It was like that sometimes; the hurt would well up until it was an overwhelming physical ache. When that happened she had to just let it have its way, let it hurt, until some of the pressure eased and she could go on.

"Can you at least tell me what in particular about the movie is so upsetting to you?"

What she wanted to do was lay her head on his shoulder and cry until there were no tears left. She wanted to be comforted like a child.

And like a woman.

"It's Lucy, you know?" She wasn't sure where the words came from. She wasn't good at this sort of thing—explaining her feelings.

She understood them perfectly. She just didn't know how to put them into words without losing the intensity in the telling.

And it was the intensity that was so hard to live with.

"What about her?"

"Her whole life." The tears continued to drip slowly

down as she spoke. Lying back against the headboard, pillows propped behind her back, Laurel shredded the tissue she held between her hands. "The aloneness. I feel it so acutely."

She studied the floral pattern on the bedspread and the threads in the quilting. Anything but look at Scott. She couldn't get that close. Couldn't have him seeing inside her.

"Because she's celebrating Christmas alone?" he asked.

"It's more than that."

"What?"

In spite of her inclination not to, she glanced over at him. He lay on his side, his head propped on his hand, watching her. His focus was so complete it was as though he was physically touching her.

"She has no one who knows her—really knows her. No one who shares a history with her, who remembers what she was like as a baby. No one who shares a single genetic trait with her. No one to belong to."

Hearing herself speak, Laurel felt ridiculous. She was weeping for a character in a movie, after all, but for her, the emotions the woman felt were very, very real.

Damaging.

"And you feel like her?"

"I just know how she feels."

It felt so odd, talking like this. It wasn't something she did. Had three and a half years of grief humbled her this much?

Or was there something about this man? Scott had changed. He'd developed an awareness and emotional maturity he'd never had before, and she felt herself opening up to him.

"You never spoke about your biological parents." He

broke into her thoughts. "Do you have any idea who they were, or what happened to them?"

The question was unexpected. It was not the kind of thing he'd ever asked before when they'd had their long discussions about life.

It also wasn't a question she answered. In the past, this was where she sidestepped, prevaricated. But something pushed her forward.

"It wasn't a classic unwed pregnancy, or even a teen pregnancy." Her instincts were screaming at her to stop before it was too late.

"My mom and dad were married." She'd never even told Paul this stuff. "My father never wanted children. Neither, from what I gleaned, did my mother. I must have been a huge mistake."

Scott moved. Staring at the bedspread, she braced herself for whatever he was going to say.

He didn't say anything.

"My father wanted my mother to have an abortion, but she didn't believe in them. They were going to give me up for adoption, but at the last minute, she decided to keep me."

How many times in her life had she wished her mother had done the kind thing and allowed her to go to a real home? To be taken in by people who wanted a new baby, who would raise her and love her all of her life?

"Apparently I cried a lot." Some things didn't change, Laurel thought with self-deprecation as she wiped her nose. "My father couldn't stand the sound."

A noise came from Scott's bed—a cross between a snort and a cough. Laurel couldn't look at him.

She was flying all over the place inside herself. Afraid. Jumbled. And far too needy. More than anything she hated being needy.

"My mom and dad were very much in love," she said quietly, the words accompanied by a deep pressure in her chest. "The only time they ever fought was about me."

Scott moved again. He must have sat up, because in her peripheral vision she could see his jeans-covered legs against the side of the bed, reaching down toward the floor.

"He finally gave her an ultimatum. Either I went, or he had to. He'd tried to accept me, because my mother thought it was their duty, but he just couldn't take my constant whining." She hadn't meant to whine. She hadn't even really known what whining was. "She chose him."

Tears dripped slowly down cheeks that were already stiff and salty. She'd long since given up wiping them away.

And she knew now why she'd never told this story before. Hearing it out loud made it that much more humiliating.

"She took me to the police, told them that she couldn't raise me, that she was afraid she was going to hurt me. I was placed in a foster home that very night and never saw her again."

The mattress she was lying on depressed, and her body tilted slightly sideways. She could see Scott's hip as he sat down, his arm as he leaned back against the headboard. For one hallucinatory second she thought he'd read her mind. That he was going to pull her up against him, offer his shoulder and let her cry.

Even the sure knowledge that it would be out of pity didn't make her any less determined to accept the invitation. She was a beggar. She'd take anything.

He reached for her hand.

"How do you know all this?" he asked softly.

"What does it matter?"

"I just can't believe someone would be cruel enough to tell a child that her mother dropped her off and left her."

The child he was talking about sounded so pathetic it made her sick. That was her. She made herself sick.

Talking about her past had been the absolute worst decision she'd ever made.

"No one told me." She tried to get angry, or at least to pretend she didn't care. "I was there. I heard them talking. Fighting. Many times. I heard what he said. What my mother said. And I was standing there holding her hand when she took me in to leave me with the authorities."

Just as Scott was holding her hand now.

"How old were you?"

"Four, almost five."

She heard him suck in a breath and waited for his response. But there was only silence.

"I was too old to be readily adopted. Most families want babies they can name and raise the way they feel best right from the beginning."

Laurel watched the movie credits scroll up the television screen, and then listened to the pervading silence. She could feel Scott's hand still holding hers.

"She had to pry my fingers loose to leave me there."

He covered their locked grip with his free hand.

"They should have been sent to jail," he said at last.

There'd been a time when she might have agreed with him. But not anymore. She didn't care what happened to them. It didn't matter. They no longer mattered.

What hurt so unbearably was that they'd robbed her of any chance of belonging. Ever. She'd never have aunts and uncles and cousins. Never be surrounded by people of whom she was a part, people who accepted her simply because she was family. There was no inner circle she had the right to a place in. She was never going to have anyone tell funny stories about the dumb things she did as a kid, or pull out embarrassing childhood pictures; she was never going to have anyone who'd loved her through all the stages of growing up.

She'd had no one gather around her for her high school graduation, celebrating her victory, claiming it as part of their own. Claiming her. No one to run to when Paul had died.

Mostly she was okay with that. She was used to it now. But sometimes, like tonight, watching Lucy, she could feel all the old pain so acutely.

"It's really okay," she said aloud. "I'm healthy. I have no financial worries and a career I love. To a lot of people, I have the perfect life. I don't know why the family thing matters to me so much, and honestly, most of the time I don't even think about it. I'm incredibly thankful for what I do have. It's just that sometimes, like tonight, I get overwhelmed with the fact that no matter how much I do, it will never be enough."

"Enough for what?"

"Just like Lucy tonight, watching through the window when the family was all gathered around the bed, I'm always going to be on the outside looking in." She sat up and turned to face him. "And I'm okay with that," she said. And meant it. "It's just sometimes when I've all but forgotten and it hits me fresh, I have to take a second to get used to the idea all over again."

Scott's blue eyes burned with an intense light as he held her gaze. "You are not on the outside," he said, the words almost a whisper as they caught in his throat.

She shook her head, needing to look away. She had no

idea why she didn't. "Of course I am," she said. "I can be the nicest person, I can give everything I have to give, do kind things for people every waking moment, but none of that's going to make me belong to them. I realized that a long time ago. And other than moments like tonight, I'm fine."

"I'm sure you are," he said, and sounded as though he meant it. "But you have not always been on the outside. I know this for a fact, because it was my inner circle you occupied."

She sat there, hardly breathing, wondering if he'd just made that up.

"The minute you walked in the door at our house all those years ago, you belonged. Immediately and unconditionally. That kind of thing doesn't change. You became family to me then, Laurel. And you always will be."

She continued to meet his gaze, even when her eyes filled with tears. Then she smiled.

"Thank you."

"You don't have to thank me," he said firmly. "You filled a very important place in our lives. The day you walked in our door, you made the lives of all three Hunter men better. We needed you far more than you ever needed us."

They'd needed her, too.

Laurel liked that.

A lot.

She'd never known. She'd never realized she had a place to fill or the ability to fill it. All her life she'd viewed herself as the recipient of kindhearted charity. And even that had been a huge blessing to her.

"When Mom died, she took all the beauty in our lives with her. The ability to appreciate a painting, to care about flowers on the table, matching dishes and proper silverware. She took everything fragile and gentle from our lives. And you brought all that back to us.''

She tried to read the expression in his eyes. ''Really?''

''Really.'' He didn't blink.

''You aren't just saying that to make me feel better? Because you don't need to, you know. I really am okay.''

''I'm not just saying that.'' He held her shoulders, turned her to face him. ''Most men don't bother with the delicate things in life, Laurel. We don't have the ability to see the need for them. But we crave them just the same.''

''Any woman could have done the same thing for you.''

''No,'' he said without hesitation. ''Any woman could have put flowers on our table, but only you could bring the lilacs.''

She didn't understand.

''It was your heart, your sensitivity, your ability to love Paul, to love all of us, that hooked us. And whenever you left, the scent of lilacs lingered behind, reminding us that you were always there for us, a part of us.''

''But...''

He put a finger to her lips.

''It was you, Laurel, no one else. Your quiet reserve, your sense of humor, your occasional and completely unpredictable bursts of spontaneity, your gentleness with Dad when he got tired and cranky—everything that was you made us happy.''

It was the nicest thing anyone had ever said to her before.

She laid her head against his chest. He let her keep it there.

It was just as comforting as she'd imagined. She didn't need to cry anymore.

"I know what you mean, though," he said after a time. "When Mom died, so did all the funny stories of what we were like as little guys, the loving reminders of who we were, where we'd come from, the assurance that we'd always be together in one way or another."

Tilting her head on his chest, Laurel gazed up at him. She should feel very strange being this intimate with Scott, but all she could think about was the way he was looking at her, as if the sight of her was all he ever wanted. And his lips. They were so close to her.

Excitingly close.

Her heart started to race, her stomach to curl with heady desire as she raised her head and brought her mouth to his. Emotionally drained, she didn't think. She just acted.

His mouth was warm, not really responding, but not pulling away. He wasn't rejecting her. Still without thought, she opened her mouth to him and exploded with desire, with hunger as he answered her invitation with the aggression of a very hungry man.

Pushing her back against the pillows, he took her mouth completely, joining them in a passion-drugged kiss that refuted any familial relationship they might have shared. There was no innocence in the exchange as their tongues danced and mated, retreated and returned to mate again.

His hand slid down her neck and over her shoulder, leaving a trail of tingling desire in its wake. Her breasts ached for him, her nipples hard and wanting. She was breathing so hard she almost choked, unable to take enough air into her lungs to sustain life.

Starved for his touch, she couldn't think, couldn't choose. She could only respond. And beg silently for more.

And keep begging until there would finally be enough.

His hand cupped her breast and Laurel almost passed

out with the intensity of her desire for him, her need to have him all over her. In her. Knowing her as intimately as it was possible for one human to know another. And to still want her even then.

"You are so beautiful...."

His words penetrated the hazy fog that cocooned her, striking a chord that wasn't right. She'd heard those words before—many times—while making love.

Laurel had only had one lover in her life, one man who'd touched her this way. Who'd said those words to her.

And it hadn't been Scott.

With a sob, she wrenched away from him, horrified by what she'd done.

"I'm so sorry," she choked, tears bursting forth. She'd just come on to her lover's little brother.

One glance at Scott was all it took to make her shame complete. His eyes were wide, his mouth pinched. He must have thought he was looking at a woman he didn't know at all.

"I think you better go," she said, amazed she could get the words out clearly.

He left without a single word, and wrenching sobs exploded from Laurel's chest.

What had she done? God in heaven, what had she just done?

"SCOTT?"

Lying in his briefs, the covers pulled halfway up his thighs, Scott held the hotel phone to his ear.

"Yeah?"

He'd known who was calling the second he'd heard the ring.

"Did I wake you?"

"No." He'd been lying in the dark for more than an hour, wondering how to repair the damage he'd done.

"I can't sleep, either."

Even now, in spite of the mess they were in, Laurel's voice brought him peace.

"I..."

"You..."

They both started at once.

"Go ahead," he said. He had no idea what he'd been about to say.

"I feel terrible about what happened."

"I know."

"The thing is, I need you, Scott."

He swallowed. Those weren't the words he'd expected to hear.

"These past days, I've found something I'd forgotten I had, something I can't bear to lose again. You're the best friend I have in the world. You're my history."

"And you're mine."

"So, can we just forget what happened tonight?"

Never. "Of course."

"And things won't be weird between us in the morning?"

"No," he said, wondering how he was ever going to keep his word, but determined to do so. "We won't let them be."

"You promise?"

"Yes."

"So we're friends?"

He stared wearily at the shadow the light from the window was making on the ceiling. "Of course."

Silence hung on the line.

"I don't want to hang up," she finally said. He wasn't sure if she was laughing—or crying.

"We can talk awhile if you like." It wasn't as if he would be getting to sleep anytime soon.

"Can I ask you something?" There was an odd tone to her voice.

He braced himself. "Yeah."

"Why do you think we did…what we did…tonight?"

How in the hell did he answer that one? How could she even ask?

"I mean, I love Paul," she said. "And you're in love with some other woman. Do you think it was just what we talked about yesterday?"

The day before seemed so long ago, he could hardly remember it. "What's that?"

"About seeking solace? Do you think that's what happened tonight?"

For her. "Probably."

"Is that bad?"

"It doesn't have to be." But it was. So bad. Laurel didn't know what had really happened three and a half years ago. Or what had happened tonight, either.

"Is it wrong?"

More wrong than she'd ever know. "No. Not unless you let it be."

"No," she said, though her voice was a little hesitant. "No, I'm not going to make it into a big deal."

"Good."

"So we're okay?"

"We're okay."

"Okay."

"You get some sleep."

"Yeah, you too."

"I will. See you in the morning." He couldn't hang up, didn't want to be left alone in the darkness to fight his demons.

"Okay." Her voice was sleepy sounding, and Scott's body responded all over again, growing hard where it had no business being hard.

If he couldn't control his body's reactions, at least he could control how he responded to them.

And where Laurel was concerned, that meant doing absolutely nothing. Ever again.

He owed it to her. To himself.

And to the brother he'd killed, as well.

CHAPTER TWELVE

SCOTT AND LAUREL WERE at breakfast—plain bagels with raspberry cream cheese—when Officer Bill Murphy, Dennis Arnett's parole officer, called. He'd just arrived at work to find Scott's message. Though he was under no obligation to do so, he agreed to meet with Scott later that morning.

"So do you think he's going to tell us everything he knows about Dennis?" Laurel asked.

Nodding, Scott watched her take a bite of her bagel—and remembered how those lips had tasted the night before.

God, he ached. Now that he'd had a taste of what he'd been craving all these years, how was he ever going to survive being this close to Laurel without touching her?

"Don't tell me you had a favor to call in in Worcester, too," Laurel said.

"As luck would have it." Scott had always been lucky when it came to his job. Another reason to make his life nothing but work.

They'd stopped at a twenty-four-hour superstore earlier that morning and picked up some essentials plus a change of clothes for each of them. Laurel had put on her new jeans and white blouse in the dressing room at the store.

"Hey," she said.

He looked up. "What?"

"Thanks."

"For what?"

"For making sure things weren't weird this morning."

Oh, but they were. So weird. No matter how badly she needed his friendship, Scott knew for certain he was going to have to tell her the truth.

"No problem," he told her. They had a case to solve. Three people to find.

And then he was going to tell her.

He had a strong suspicion that every moment until then was going to be torture. And he didn't want to think what it would be like once he lost her for good.

"SCOTT, IT'S GREAT TO finally meet you," Officer Murphy said as he ushered Scott and Laurel into an interrogation room at the police station, closing the door behind them.

Laurel was silent as Scott, shaking the other man's hand, returned the compliment.

The two men talked briefly about their mutual acquaintance, an officer Scott had known in the academy who'd asked Scott to pick up Murphy's runaway niece from a truck stop outside New Ashford the previous year.

"How's she doing?" Scott asked Murphy now.

"Good, thank goodness," Murphy said, his face serious. "Every once in a while a kid gets scared straight. Kaitlin's been the model daughter and student ever since she got back. I think it helped that instead of ranting at her and slapping her with some stringent punishment my sister and her husband listened to the kid and addressed the problems that had led to Kaitlin's running away in the first place."

Scott introduced Laurel then, telling Murphy that she was an investigative reporter helping him with this unofficial investigation.

The three of them sat down on hard plastic chairs at the small table in the center of the room, an open file in front of them. Murphy gave Laurel permission to tape their session.

"So far Arnett's been a model parolee," Murphy was saying. "He checks in like clockwork. Has a job. Really seems to be sincere in his attempts to take advantage of this second chance and make a new life for himself."

"Where's he working?" Scott asked, his notebook in one hand, a pen in the other.

"For a car dealership selling new trucks, which is perfect for him. He's got the gift of gab, that man."

"The type of salesman you want to watch out for?" Laurel asked.

"That's putting it lightly." Murphy sat back in his chair, his hands in the pockets of his workday blues. "Dennis Arnett could charm the meat off a cow."

Looking at Scott, Laurel wondered if he was remembering, as she was, Katy Miller's description of Leslie Renwick's new boyfriend. Too charming. At first, it was a long-enough stretch to seem incredible, but considering the Renwicks had been one of Dennis's sister's largest clients, the idea didn't seem quite so fantastic.

Of course, if she and Scott were correct in thinking that Cecilia was Leslie's mother, that would mean Dennis Arnett was dating his own niece.

Not a pretty thought. Judging by the grim look on Scott's face he was traveling in the same negative direction as well.

"In spite of some very prominent strikes against him, I have high hopes for Arnett," Murphy was saying. "He settled right down as soon as he came to town. Even has a girlfriend. As far as I can tell, he's been with the same woman for the entire time he's been here."

Scott pulled out a picture Katy Miller had given them. Laurel's chest filled with dread.

"This isn't her, is it?" he asked, his gaze intense as he watched for the other man's reaction.

"That's her, all right," Murphy said, leaning forward with a frown. "What does she have to do with you?"

"We think she's missing."

As Scott filled Officer Murphy in on what they'd found out so far, starting from the call he'd received to investigate a possible missing person, Laurel wondered how much longer they were going to be able to keep kidding themselves that William was going to be fine.

Something was very, very wrong.

"You said earlier that Arnett had some prominent strikes against him," Scott stated minutes later. "What did you mean by that?"

Murphy was still frowning. "He's a repeat offender for one, though this last stint was the first time he'd ever spent any real length of time behind bars. First time to actually make it to prison."

"Let me guess, his family was able to buy his way out of trouble before that."

"From what I can ascertain." Murphy nodded.

"So what else?" Scott persisted. "You said strikes as in plural."

Sliding a sideways glance at Laurel, Murphy hesitated, but only for a moment. "There was some...uh...trouble when he first got to prison...."

"Trouble that he created? Or the 'virgin blood meets hardened criminal' variety?"

"The latter. Arnett was in a spot of trouble one night, but before anything happened, one of the other guys was there. Saved his ass, from what I understand."

"No pun intended?"

Murphy shrugged.

"So why is this a bad thing?"

"Arnett and the guy were seen together a lot after that. And Carl Nevil is not a man anyone's mama would pick to be her kid's friend. Too much time spent with him would lead anyone astray. He's one of New York's more famous crime giants—been in and out of prison more times than I've changed shoes. I hear he was just sent up for murder last year. And this time it should be for good."

"Did you say Carl Nevil?"

Laurel glanced sharply at Scott. He'd sounded odd. Like he was trying not to choke.

"Yeah, you know of him?"

"Maybe." Scott's answer was vague, but there was nothing vague about his response to this interview. He was really bothered.

And that bothered Laurel most of all.

THERE WAS NO JOKE-TELLING that afternoon. And no more leads, either. Officer Murphy had given them the address of Dennis's apartment—an old house he was renting, or half a house, to be precise. Dennis's apartment had been renovated, while the other side of the house stood in vacant disrepair, waiting its turn.

No one answered Arnett's door when they knocked, so they made a quick tour of the yard.

"At least Leslie's car isn't in the garage," Laurel said as they stood on the front lawn, which needed a good mowing, and looked up at the vacant house. There was no sign of life anywhere. No junk mail. No newspapers.

They went to the car dealership next. Laurel wasn't really surprised to hear that Dennis Arnett wasn't there. The people she and Scott looked for were never where they were supposed to be.

"He worked on Saturday morning," the sales manager told them. "We traditionally run a big sale this time of year and the entire front end of the dealership is required to work. He's been off the last few days but he's scheduled for the three to nine o'clock shift today. You folks friends of his?"

"Friends of the family," Scott said, his jaw tense. "We'll stop in later."

"Can I give him a message?" The manager followed them out to the parking lot.

Thanking him for his offer, Scott explained that they were from out of town and it would be easier if they checked back in themselves. When they did, they found that Dennis hadn't shown up for work that day.

Scott called Murphy to report the news. While Arnett was not required to let his parole officer know if he was going to miss a day's work, he was required to stay in town. And to let Murphy know where he was staying.

"It looks like Arnett might be violating his parole," he told Laurel as he dropped the cell phone into the console between them. He sat in the parking lot at the dealership, staring straight ahead. "Why does this not surprise me?"

Laurel wished there was something she could do to make things better for him. They paid another visit to Leslie's after they left the dealership, but it proved to be equally futile.

They'd reached a standstill. If Arnett didn't return, they were going to have to wait for his next meeting with Murphy two days later to question him.

If he showed up.

All in all, it had been a tough day.

AS SHE AND SCOTT FINISHED dinner in a diner close to the motel, Laurel really started to lose hope. She just couldn't come up with a good reason for William Byrd not to have at least called Twin Oaks to say he'd been delayed somewhere.

Or to explain why his car was at Cecilia's, but he wasn't; and Cecilia's car was at Leslie's, but she wasn't.

"There was a park just a couple blocks from the motel," she said as they exited the restaurant. "Would you mind taking a walk with me?"

As tired as she was, she knew the fatigue was more mental than physical. The thought of sitting alone in the motel room with nothing to do was not the least bit appealing.

And inviting Scott in was out of the question.

"Lead the way," he said. "I'd be glad for the exercise."

Moonlight lit the park better than streetlights could have, but it wasn't a place Laurel would have wanted to be alone that late at night. Yet with Scott she felt perfectly safe. Energized, even.

"You have days like today fairly regularly, don't you?" she asked him.

"Afraid so."

"How do you keep it from getting to you? I keep thinking about William and Cecilia, what might be happening to them—or what's already happened—and I get a sick feeling in my stomach."

"It gets to me, but I've learned to channel my thoughts."

His voice was strong in the darkness. Reassuring.

"To what?"

"I just focus on finding the answers. The sooner I do, the sooner the suffering stops, one way or the other."

It was what Laurel had been trying to do most of the

afternoon. Unfortunately she couldn't control her thoughts the way Scott did. She envied him that.

They walked silently for a bit. The park was deserted except for the two of them, making Laurel feel that they were all alone in the world—a feeling she didn't mind at all. Swing sets, monkey bars, a sandbox were all just shadowy shapes in the night.

"I saw you making a phone call when we stopped for gas this afternoon." Scott's voice, though soft, consumed her in the darkness.

"Yeah." She'd thought he was in the men's room.

"Were you calling the station?"

"No."

"Who, then?'

She felt guilty as hell. "A friend."

"Someone you know well?"

"Fairly well."

"Someone you spend a lot of time with?"

"A fair amount." *Fair. Fairly.* She needed to find another word. There was nothing fair about any of this.

A light breeze swept over them and Laurel shivered.

"A man?"

She didn't want to do this and felt incredibly disloyal. "Yes."

"Does he have a name?"

"Shane."

"You're dating him?" She couldn't tell if the odd note in Scott's voice was her own paranoid imagination or really there.

"Not really."

"How do you not really date someone?"

Darting off the sidewalk, Laurel ran across the grass. "Let's swing," she called to Scott, sitting down in one of the black leather straps, grabbing hold of the chains with both hands and pushing off.

Instead of joining her, racing to see who could get the highest as he might have done in their other life, Scott stood behind her, gently pushing her.

"You didn't answer my question," he said after a time.

"We spend most of our free time together," she said slowly, trying to explain something she didn't really understand herself. "Go to movies, to the theater, to dinner."

"Sounds like dating to me."

She shook her head. "It's mostly platonic."

"He's gay?" Scott sounded so serious, Laurel laughed. And was ridiculously flattered, too. As though a man couldn't be with her and not want her in a romantic sense.

"No, he's not gay," she said.

"And he's never tried anything?" He sounded as if such a thing weren't even possible.

And Laurel liked that implication so much it scared her.

"He's tried," she said, struggling to think about Shane, not Scott. She knew what this thing with Scott was all about. They'd figured it out the night before. She was looking for solace. That was all.

"He's even succeeded some."

"And he wants more," Scott guessed.

Laurel sailed higher, peaking for a second before coming down.

"It's part of the reason I'm here," she told him, once again being more open with him than was her way.

Things were changing. Within her. Around her. Nothing was making sense.

He pushed her a couple of times but said nothing. Each time she felt his hands on her back, she tingled with awareness. And was too needy to make him stop.

"Shane wants me to sleep with him."

"That's bold for a man you aren't even dating."

Even if she'd missed the sarcasm in his remark, Laurel couldn't ignore the much harder push against her back. Scott disapproved.

Because of Paul?

Because Shane had asked her to sleep with him, not marry him?

She was grateful for the breeze that cooled her heated skin.

"It's been more than three years," she said, defending her actions—to herself as much as to him. "If I'm going to have any kind of life, I have to get over Paul. Move on."

"That's not reason enough to start sleeping with someone."

That's exactly what she'd been telling herself, but...

"Unless Paul is the only reason I'm hesitating."

The swing was slowing as Scott's pushes grew gentler. "Is he?"

"I don't know."

The swing had all but stopped. Scott sat down next to her.

"Do you think he is?"

She drew an arc in the sand with her foot. The rough grains filled her sandal, sliding uncomfortably between her toes. "I did."

"Past tense?"

"I really like Shane a lot, admire him, respect him," she said. "I enjoy our time together. The fact that he's great looking doesn't hurt, either."

"So what's the problem?"

She hesitated a moment before answering. "Anytime I think about going to bed with him, anytime he tries to get closer…physically…than we already have been, I feel trapped. I thought it was because of guilt over Paul.''

''So what changed?''

Safe in the darkness, Laurel couldn't hold back the truth. Only Scott could help her put it in its right place—help her understand. ''I didn't feel trapped last night.''

''You were horrified.''

''You're Paul's brother.''

''I'm aware of that.''

''I'm deathly afraid I'm transferring my feelings for him onto you.''

''Were you thinking of Paul when you kissed me?''

Heat flooded her face, her body. ''No.''

''How about when I kissed you back?''

He twisted her swing around to face him, holding her steady with his legs outside hers. ''To tell you the truth,'' he said, emphasizing each word with a squeeze on the outside of her thighs, ''I'm flattered.''

Desire curled inside her so fiercely she didn't have time to slow it down. To control it.

Leaning forward, Laurel touched his lips with hers, just like she'd been thinking about doing since she'd tasted him the night before.

This wasn't right. It wasn't fair.

But she couldn't seem to stop herself. Wanting Scott was the first bit of powerful feeling she'd had since Paul was killed.

His lips were soft against hers. Undemanding—and yet responsive, too. He didn't take over this time…wasn't the least bit aggressive.

And yet, as her lips played over his, her hands resting on his thighs, he was right there with her all the way. Letting her coax him. Kissing her back.

With a boldness she'd never known before, her tongue

played with Scott, running lightly along his lips, pushing between them, teasing his tongue.

He let her play, answering every move, instigating none. Turning her on, driving her crazy, making her want him more and more.

One hand slid higher on his thigh as she slipped in the swing. And then it moved higher because she wanted it to. Her fingers were at the juncture of his thigh, resting next to his groin.

This was Scott. Strong, confident Scott. And she wanted more.

Deepening the kiss from playful to serious, Laurel lost herself in the desire she'd built. Fire burned all through her as she left her hand just shy of complete intimacy on his thigh. His jeans were stretched taut and she was pretty sure her finger was resting against an erection. For her.

She literally ached with wanting him, but he didn't move. Didn't say a word. Didn't touch her back.

"Scott?" she whispered, her hand trembling.

"Yeah?" His voice sounded as though he hadn't used it in years.

"You okay?"

She wanted to look up at him but couldn't quite do it. Instead, she closed her eyes.

"Yeah."

"You want me to stop?" she asked.

"Not unless you want to."

She didn't. She left her hand there, not moving. Teetering on the brink of something she knew she could never discover yet wanted to so badly.

What she wanted was to feel the velvet of his skin. And more. She wanted it all.

But it was for solace, she reminded herself. And she couldn't make love for solace.

Her hand slid off his leg.

Grabbing her around the neck, Scott kissed her—hard. Then he stood, turning away.

They walked back to the motel side by side and said good-night outside their respective doors.

Neither of them said a word about what had just happened.

CHAPTER THIRTEEN

"IT'S ANOTHER DAY AND A HALF until Dennis is due to meet with Murphy, so what do you say we head back to Cooper's Corner and show his picture around there?" Scott asked Laurel the second she stepped out of her door the next morning. His plan was double-edged. Not only did he need to get to Maureen and see if she recognized Arnett from any old pictures in her dossier on Carl Nevil, but he needed some time away from Laurel.

"Sure beats hanging around here looking at deserted homes," Laurel said.

As hard as he tried, he couldn't get last night out of his mind. Just the sight of her hand on the strap of her bag was driving him insane. He recalled that hand on his body...on his thigh...

With clenched jaw, Scott moved up to the motel desk, paid their bills and pocketed his wallet. He couldn't do this. Couldn't continue to be what Laurel needed—a perfect friend who was there for her if she needed him.

That was who he wanted to be. But he wasn't perfect. He wasn't really even a friend—not by his definition. He hadn't been honest with her or loyal to either Laurel or his brother. And he couldn't be there for her, either.

He was going to have to tell her the truth about his feelings for her all those years. About Paul's death. There was nothing he could do to change things. No way he could go back and fix everything.

And he was going to do his job. The lives of three people could be in danger. William Byrd, Cecilia Hamilton and possibly Leslie Renwick. And now, if Nevil was somehow involved, after all, the Coopers' lives could be at risk as well. Or their livelihood at the very least.

This was something he was good at. This was where he could make a difference. He needed to concentrate his efforts on solving this case.

While they had their morning coffee and bagels, Laurel also seemed determined to concentrate on the case. She had her little tape recorder out, documenting every word they said.

"Don't you find it odd that Dennis is missing, too?" she asked. "That every single person we try to find in this case has disappeared?"

"If nothing else, it makes things more difficult."

He took a sip of coffee, wishing he'd asked for less cream.

"So, in light of the fact that Dennis is Leslie's new boyfriend, you want to rethink the possibility that Cecilia is her mother?"

That hand, holding her napkin. Last night it had been touching him...

"I'd like to, but I'm not convinced we can. There's nothing that says Dennis knows about Leslie and Cecilia."

She took a bite of bagel, licking the cream cheese off her upper lip.

"I just don't think Leslie's in cahoots with Dennis. Katy's a good woman and she seems too fond of Leslie for Leslie to be involved in something criminal."

"Bad people fool good people every day." He should have had them put some Jack Daniel's in the coffee.

"So you think we've got a double blackmail going on?"

"I don't know what to think." He was really bothered by Dennis's absence on top of everything else. He was missing something vital. Something that would make sense out of all four players together. Why had William and Cecilia gone to visit Leslie? He just couldn't get that to make sense.

Scott's gut tightened. "What hunches are we the most sure about?"

Laurel glanced up. She hadn't looked him in the eye all morning. "Cecilia is most likely Leslie's mother."

"Right."

"William was using that knowledge to blackmail her for his half of the company."

Scott thought about that possibility. "I'll go with that."

"Dennis is dating Leslie."

Was this what they'd left themselves with? Scott wondered. Business talk over cups of coffee with no personal connection at all. Nothing like the intimate conversation they'd had the morning before.

"And Cecilia didn't let her assistant know that her brother was out of jail," he said, deciding to leave his bagel. He'd only ordered it out of habit. "I wonder if that means she didn't know?"

"I wondered that, too," Laurel said. "But it doesn't make much sense, does it? He knows she'd help him, and when would he need it more than after ten years of being locked up?"

Scott didn't have the answer to that.

"Maybe they're all just having some weird family reunion," Laurel said, wiping her mouth one last time before throwing down her napkin.

"You ready?" He was tired of sitting there. Tired of

watching that damn hand holding the napkin. Taking the bagel to her lips. Wrapping itself around her coffee cup.

And tired of knowing that William Byrd and Cecilia Hamilton were out in the world someplace, most likely needing help that they weren't getting.

TALK OF THE CASE DIDN'T LAST them very long once they were on the road. Laurel tried to get Scott to talk to her about other things. The towns they were passing. The changes she'd noticed in Cooper's Corner. She'd turned so she was facing him again—not that it did her much good.

He wasn't looking at her. Laurel knew she was going to have to do something about that. She just didn't know what.

Staring out the window at the village off to their right, she wondered what it would be like to live there. She thought of the mothers in those houses baking cookies, playing games with their children. Gardening.

"Are you angry with me?" she asked.

"No."

"Honestly?"

"Honestly," he replied, staring straight ahead. "I'm not the least bit angry with you," he said, emphasizing on that last word.

"Who are you angry with?"

"Nobody. Myself, maybe."

"What have you done to be angry at yourself?"

He shifted, lifting his foot from the gas pedal as he did so. Laurel's eye was drawn to the movement, to the muscled thigh closest to her.

"I'm not angry."

"Then why do you sound that way?"

Scott sighed and shook his head. "Now's not the time."

If she'd thought it would do any good, she'd have continued badgering him until he was truthful with her. Instead she let the subject drop, promising herself she'd pursue it again later. Hopefully they'd have time to talk that night.

She couldn't imagine what Scott had done to bring that tight-lipped look to his face or the unemotional tone to his voice. But she wasn't going to rest until she found out.

Her mind wandered to William and Cecilia, wondering how much rest they'd had in the past few days. Did they really hate each other? Had Cecilia loved William's father, or was it his money she'd married? For all their searching, all she and Scott had so far was a series of disjointed clues.

"I'm sorry." She didn't want to think about William and Cecilia—not until there was something more they could do. She didn't want to think about either of them defenseless, in trouble. And Leslie. What if she didn't know Dennis was her uncle? *If* Dennis was her uncle. Who was the bad guy in all this? And who were just innocent pawns in an evil game?

"Sorry for what?" Scott had both hands on the wheel.

"Last night." She'd been trying all morning to bring that up. It had to be what was bothering him. He'd been fine until she'd lost her mind and…

"You have nothing to be sorry about."

"But…"

"Laurel—" his voice was sharp "—let it go."

"I can't…"

Finally he turned to look at her, and she wished he hadn't. There was something in Scott's eyes she'd never seen before. Resignation. Hopelessness. "Right now," he said, "neither can I."

She had no idea what that meant, but she couldn't ask. He was like a stranger, sitting there.

Bereft, a little bit frightened, Laurel searched frantically for a way to fix things. As she sat there, finding it hard to breathe, she knew only one thing for sure. She had to find a way to get the old Scott back.

She couldn't imagine living life without him.

AS IT TURNED OUT, LAUREL and Scott made another turn around Cooper's Corner together before they headed up the hill to Twin Oaks. This time, rather than just one picture, they had four to show around—William, Cecilia, Leslie and Dennis.

The results were exactly the same. Nothing. Except for a couple of people who'd been working at the diner, pretty much everyone had been at the Founders Day barbecue. And though they did have another confirmation from a waitress at the diner that William and Cecilia had had a late lunch together, no one had seen either Dennis Arnett or Leslie Renwick.

Back at Twin Oaks, while Laurel went upstairs to freshen up and see if the twins were awake from their afternoon nap, Scott took the opportunity to have a moment alone with Maureen in her office. He and Laurel had already filled she and her brother in on the new developments in the case, but Scott had some private business he needed to discuss with the ex-NYPD detective.

The first thing she wanted to know, of course, was if there had been any word on Owen Nevil.

Scott shook his head. "His sources say he could be gone as long as a week or two, mountain trekking in the wilderness. They claim they have no way to reach him and weren't even sure where he'd gone, though he tended to favor the Appalachians. After his time in prison, the wilderness appealed to him.''

"Do you believe them?"

Hands in the pockets of his slacks, Scott shrugged. "There could be some truth to the cabin fever bit—being cooped up in a four-by-ten cell could give anyone claustrophobia…''

"…and it's also one hell of a convenient alibi.''

He couldn't argue with her there.

"I need you to look at this picture." Scott pulled the photo of Dennis Arnett out of his shirt pocket. "You recognize him?"

Ponytail falling over her shoulder, Maureen leaned forward to take a thorough look.

"Yeah," she said almost immediately. "Who is he?"

Scott's stomach plummeted. "You knew him in New York?"

It was going to turn out that the Nevils were involved after all, and things were going to get a hell of a lot worse before they got better.

"No," Maureen surprised him by saying. "I ran into him, literally, on the evening of the Founders Day barbecue. I'd come back to Twin Oaks to get the kids' sweaters and stopped in town to put a couple of letters in the mailbox so they'd go out first thing Monday morning. He was coming up the street so fast he didn't see me. Nearly ran me over. Who is he?" she asked again, frowning. She took one more long look at the photo as she handed it back.

"Dennis Arnett."

"Cecilia's brother?"

"The very same."

"And you think he had something to do with William's disappearance?"

"Seems pretty likely."

Leaning back against the closed office door, arms folded across his chest, Scott hated to bring up the rest.

"He's thick with Carl Nevil," he said softly.

"Oh, God."

"I guess Carl saved Arnett from some bad stuff when Arnett was first sent up."

"You said that was more than ten years ago."

"Right."

"They've been friends for a long time."

"And you know how guys can bond in prison."

"Oh, God."

"Don't panic yet," Scott reassured Maureen. "This really could be a coincidence."

"And how many times have you seen that happen since you've been on the force, Detective?" Maureen asked, her shoulders straight as she looked Scott in the eye.

"Not many." He paused. "But there were some."

They all just had to hope like hell that this was one of those times.

Either that or the situation was even more grim than he'd feared. If the Nevils were involved and this was all some nefarious plot to wreak revenge on Maureen Maguire, not only were at least three of Scott's four missing persons likely to end up dead, but the Coopers' futures didn't look good, either.

IT WAS ANOTHER LONG DAY. Laurel called the station, extending her vacation. Because she hadn't taken much time off since she'd started there, they didn't give her a hard time about the change of plans. At that point, she wouldn't have cared if they had. As much as she loved her job, this time with Scott was a lifeline, and finding William Byrd had become a need far greater than earning money. Besides, her boss was eager for her to continue with her investigation, since it was looking more and more like she was going to have one hell of a story.

She just wasn't sure if it was going to be human interest or a murder story.

BY DINNERTIME, HAVING exhausted every idea they had for follow-up in Cooper's Corner, Scott and Laurel decided to head back to Worcester. At least there they could keep a watch on both Dennis's and Leslie's deserted homes and be close by in case Dennis contacted Officer Murphy.

"Two people just can't vanish into thin air," Laurel said, frustrated, hot and tired as they pulled into a motel in Worcester later that night.

"No, though they could hide out for a long time...."

"Or be hidden."

"It's beginning to look more like that's what's happening," Scott said.

It was what she'd been thinking, but it still scared her to hear him put her fears into words. The only other alternative was far worse.

That they were dead.

"For ransom?"

"Possibly, though I would have thought Hamilton Lending would have received some kind of demands by now if that were the case. Besides, there's the million dollars that's already been taken from Cecilia's account."

Following him in to get rooms for the night, Laurel shivered. William, Cecilia, Leslie. Were they together?

"Scott?" she asked as they crossed the lobby. She

knew if she waited any longer—until she had a room to run to and hide—she'd chicken out.

"Yeah?"

He was the stranger still—that pleasant but distant man who'd looked at her infrequently that day. The one who was freezing her out of the most valuable friendship of her life.

"After we get settled in our rooms, I need to talk to you, okay?"

He surprised her by agreeing at once. "Sure I need to talk to you, too."

That didn't sound good.

THE EVENING WAS COOL, pleasant. They decided to walk around the corner where they'd seen a deli and pick up sandwiches for dinner. They ate them under a tree in a field across the street from the motel. It felt good to Laurel to be outside, and now that it was getting dark, the night surrounded them in a cocoon of anonymity.

She took a deep breath, knowing she couldn't continue to avoid the difficult conversation ahead of her. She'd done Scott a horrible disservice the night before. Somehow she had to make that right.

She loved Paul.

But wanted Scott.

Even now, after an entire day of being shut out, an entire day of knowing that what she'd done was wrong, she wanted him.

Just thinking about the night before when Scott had allowed her to touch him so intimately, her belly curled with desire. And when she thought of Paul, her heart filled with love.

"I don't know what's the matter with me." They were

through eating, leaning back against the tree, shoulders touching.

He was engrossed with a blade of grass, smoothing it between thumb and forefinger, watching it curl. "What makes you think something's wrong with you?"

She took a deep breath. "Last night."

"You don't…"

"Let me finish." She hadn't meant the words to be so loud. "I'm in love with Paul," she admitted flatly, almost wishing that when she looked, she'd find her fiancé missing from her heart so she would be free.

She'd never expected to think that, to want that, but she did. Fresh shame engulfed her.

"There's nothing wrong with that."

"But for some reason, I want you so desperately I'm thinking about…being with you…all the time."

She was glad for the falling night, the fact that they weren't facing each other. Speaking out to the open field made the humiliating confession possible.

He raised one knee, and rested a forearm across it, but said nothing.

"If it were just sex, I'd understand," she said, thinking things through as she talked. "It's been three and a half years, we've been in close proximity the last few days, there's the fact that you're an almost perfect specimen of manhood…"

"*Almost* perfect?"

Laurel heard the grin in his voice and the constriction in her chest loosened a little.

"There is that ego of yours," she teased. He *was* perfect. But he didn't need her to tell him that. In high school and college he'd had every girl he'd ever wanted—and many he didn't—swarming after him.

Paul had been too focused on his goals to be aware of

the lovely coeds around him. Focused on his goals—and on Laurel.

"But it's not just sex?" he asked softly, seriously.

Shaking her head, Laurel tried to explain what she didn't understand. "It's like I'm desperate to be close to you. And there's nothing closer than sex. The thought of sharing that with you makes me feel safe."

"Safe from what?"

She didn't know.

"Are you afraid of something? Has someone threatened you? This Shane, maybe?"

"No."

"So why safe?"

"Safe from losing you, maybe." She picked her own piece of grass. "I don't know."

"So it's not desire you feel, but some need to stay connected?"

"No." She could feel her face burning and was glad he couldn't see that. "I definitely feel desire." And then, because she was being completely honest with him, she added, "Like I've never felt before in my life."

The words fell baldly into the night air and hung there, suspended.

"What about Paul?"

"Not even with him."

What was the matter with her? Being more turned on by Scott than she ever had been by his older brother was beyond transference. How could you transfer what hadn't been there to begin with?

There was no movement beside her. If not for Scott's warmth making her nerves crawl with anticipation, she'd have wondered if he'd left.

"It's okay, you know." Her throat was dry. Too dry. "I didn't tell you this to put you on the spot or make you feel like you have to tell me you feel something, too. I just wanted to explain why I was so out of line last night. And to apologize.''

"I told you earlier today that you have no reason to apologize for anything.''

"My behavior was inappropriate to the point of insulting.''

"It was flattering.''

It was her turn to say nothing. She was too busy trying to pull a breath past the tightness in her chest.

"You didn't have me at gunpoint last night, Laurel,'' Scott said, his voice soft but completely sure. "I could have said no at any time.''

"So why didn't you?''

"Because the pleasure was so excruciating, I couldn't deny myself.'' Before she could figure out what to say, he continued. "Because after dreaming of something like that happening for so many years, I didn't have the strength to stop you.''

Her insides were on fire. "Oh. Then...''

"And because I knew that it was something that wasn't ever going to be my right to enjoy.''

"But...''

"I killed Paul, Laurel. It's my fault the man you love is lying in a grave instead of in bed beside you every night.''

CHAPTER FOURTEEN

LAUREL FLINCHED BESIDE HIM. "You know that's not true."

"I know that it is." His voice was gravelly, jarring in the peaceful night air.

Laurel turned, leaning her shoulder right next to his against the tree, her face only inches away, torturing him with its promise of a sweetness he could never receive. He could feel her looking at him and was glad for the darkness that allowed him blindness, an excuse to avoid the compassion he knew he'd read in those expressive gray eyes.

"I took a grief class, Scott, and it's natural for you to blame yourself for living when Paul died—especially when you were driving the car—but it was not your fault. The car slid on a patch of ice. There was nothing anyone could do."

She was repeating most of what he'd told her that day in the churchyard—he just hadn't mentioned who'd been driving. He hadn't realized she'd even heard him that day. And now he knew for sure that she hadn't seen an accident report.

The car had slid on some ice. And there'd been nothing anyone could do after that. It was *before* the accident that things should have been done differently.

Stars were out now, twinkling a promise so far away he wondered how he'd ever believed in wishing on them.

"I wasn't driving the car."

"Of course you were. You and Paul both promised me when you went to Boston for that party that you'd do all the driving. Paul was a horrible winter driver. And it was your car."

"I know. But I wasn't driving."

"I don't understand." He heard the confusion in her voice. She was so certain he and Paul wouldn't lie to her. Her trust was that complete.

Another thing for him to destroy.

"I got drunk at the bachelor party," he confessed. "Disgustingly, falling-down, passing-out drunk."

"You don't drink."

"I know."

"You never got drunk. Not in high school. Or college."

"I know."

"So…"

He was going to have to tell her. Right then. He struggled to find the right words.

"I got so drunk I stripped down to my briefs, stood on a table and sang karaoke."

He'd hoped she'd laugh, that maybe they could bring a little levity into the conversation. Her silence told him what he'd already known. There was absolutely nothing funny about any of this.

Head down, he picked at blades of grass that were only shadows. "I was aiming for oblivion."

"But why?"

The bitch of it was, he'd found neither. He could, still this night, remember every excruciating moment.

"The party ended at two in the morning. Up in my room, I pretended it was still going on. I turned on music videos and danced with a bottle until about four."

"You had to leave for Cooper's Corner at six."

"I know."

"You didn't know what time it was?"

"I knew." Every single minute that had ticked by was a minute closer to a life he couldn't stomach thinking about—a life with Laurel as Paul's wife.

As it turned out, the minutes were ticking away the last hours of Paul's life.

"When Paul knocked on the door at six, I was sitting on the bathroom floor, thinking about getting sick."

"Why, Scott?" Blame had not yet replaced confusion. "Why would you do such a thing to yourself? It doesn't make sense."

It made hellishly perfect sense.

"I was in no state to stand, let alone drive," he continued. "I told Paul that we'd promised you he wouldn't drive, but he figured you'd be more mad at him for missing his wedding. He figured that if I slept for the three-hour drive home, I'd be sober enough by the time we hit Pittsfield for us to switch drivers."

"That doesn't sound like Paul."

"He wasn't going to miss his wedding."

"Had he been drinking, too?"

"Not nearly as much as I had."

"But he'd been drinking."

He didn't want to remember. Paul had been so happy, the alcohol and the excitement of his wedding freeing him from his usual restraint.

"Some."

"Paul didn't drink, either."

She couldn't think badly of Paul. Period.

"He was just happy, Laurel, happier than I've ever seen him. The guys poured him a shot or two and for once he threw caution to the wind and joined in the fun."

"I wish I could have seen that."

"Yeah." He wished the memory didn't have so much pain attached to it for him.

They both fell silent, but it wasn't over yet.

"So he was hungover, too."

"Not really."

"Paul wasn't used to drinking."

Okay. So maybe Paul had been a little worse for wear.

"He'd had four hours to sleep it off."

Laurel turned around, her back against the tree once more. Pulling her knees up, she wrapped her arms around them, rubbing her legs from her ankles to her knees, back and forth, slowly, as though easing a pain.

It was a pain that couldn't be eased. Scott knew. He'd tried every way he could think of, but nothing worked.

"So you were sleeping when he hit that patch of ice."

"Yes."

A car drove by. Scott wondered where the occupant was going, and wished he were going there, too. Anywhere would be better than this.

"You said the seat belt broke."

She'd heard that, too. All these years he'd comforted himself with the fact that she'd been in shock that morning, that it would all be a blur to her—nothing to haunt her nights the way his had been haunted.

Images of waking up in the car, hearing the sirens, the hissing of steam, the voices yelling outside his window. Getting out, stumbling around the car until he recognized that it was his car, wondering why he'd been so far from the steering wheel. Coming upon Paul's body... Remembering where they'd been going. What Scott had done.

"The seat belt on the driver's side broke," he told her now, wishing he felt as emotionless as he sounded. "The one on the passenger side didn't. That's why I lived and he didn't. Being thrown from the car is what killed him."

"And because you should have been driving, it's your fault he was killed and not you."

Damn. Who would have thought, after all the recriminating things he'd said to himself, it would hurt so much to hear her say those words?

"Yes."

"Bullshit."

She must not have understood. He'd have to figure out a way to make it clear to her.

"That seat belt breaking was an act of fate, Scott," she went on. "It could just as easily have been the passenger belt that broke."

Wrong.

"I'd had a recall notice on it. Three of them."

"On the driver's side belt."

That was the one.

"I'd already taken the damn thing in for a recall on a floor mat—one had doubled up under a gas pedal and caused an accident. And I'd had it in for a fuel-system recall that had turned out to be nothing more than an indicator light."

"So you didn't bother to take it in for the seat belt."

"I was going to…"

Maybe. When he'd had the thing serviced the next time.

"If this is true, you could have sued the company."

"For my own lack of responsibility?" he asked derisively. "Why should they pay for that? And what were they going to be able to do to make amends for my having killed my brother? Bring him back?"

"Of course not."

Arms still around her shins, she laid her head on her knees. After a while he wondered if she'd fallen asleep.

He leaned his own head back against the tree, reluctant to disturb her.

"Why did you get so drunk?"

Her words were like a knife jabbing into him.

"What was bothering you so badly the night before Paul died?" she persisted.

Scott needed to move. To stretch. His joints ached from sitting on the hard ground for so long.

He couldn't move.

"I..."

"I have to know what was driving you, Scott." Her tone brooked no argument. "I *have* to know..." The words dwindled off to a whisper as her voice broke.

She was crying.

With a sick feeling in his gut he realized that she'd been sitting there all this time, quietly crying.

"Because it seemed like the only way to forget how much I hated myself."

She turned her head toward him. "Hated yourself?" Her mouth was so close he could feel her breath on the side of his face.

"Yeah."

"You were the best man in your brother's wedding and were throwing him a bachelor party. You'd just gotten word about the job in Boston. You were getting a nice raise, a promotion, a new home close to your family. A new life. One you'd earned through hard work and sacrifice. What did you have to hate yourself for?"

For a second there, hearing her describe his life, he actually felt good about himself and was tempted to leave well enough alone.

"I hated myself for being in love with my brother's fiancée." The words were cold, unemotional. It was the best he could do for himself, because he couldn't stop there. "I hated myself for being so damned jealous of him that I couldn't be happy for him. For hating how happy he was, knowing that making you exclusively his was the root of that happiness.''

She didn't move. Didn't say anything. And then, slowly, her head turned away from him and she gazed out at the field in front of her.

"It had to just be the moment, the situation. Paul was getting married. You were there for every step of the planning, reminding him he had decisions to make when he was too focused on work to remember. Sometimes it seemed more like you were the groom than he was. It's natural that you'd superimpose his feelings onto your own in the end.''

She'd given him an out. Scott considered taking it.

"It wasn't just that night.''

"So, it was just those last weeks of planning, when everything was so crazy and you and I were spending so much time together getting everything finalized while Paul finished that embezzlement case.'' She sounded adamant in spite of her shaking voice.

He could go with that. Should go with that. No one would ever know.

"No.''

"How long?'' The voice no longer sounded like hers. It was flat. Distant.

"What?''

"How long were you…feeling…like that?''

"Since high school.''

. Her head snapped around. "No way, Scott. You've built this up into something that's not even there,'' she said, her voice breathy with relief. "You were in love in high school, that's true. About ten times. Always with beautiful blondes who thought you could solve any problem, make any wrong right. They hung all over you— adored you.''

"You're blond."

She faced the field again. "Yes, but..."

"And you, more than anyone, spent hours talking to me about solving all of the world's problems."

"Yes, but..."

"Didn't you ever wonder why I never had a serious girlfriend? Why I've never, not once, dated a girl more than twice?"

"Because you had so many to choose from and weren't ready to settle down?"

"Wrong." He turned to look at her, knowing that he was going to feel damned humiliated when this was over, but needing to finish now that he'd started. "It was because no one measured up to you."

She shook her head. "No."

"Yes."

"I can't accept that."

He didn't blame her. Neither could he.

And there was one more thing he couldn't accept. Not ever. Not in this life and not in any that were to come.

"Right before the bachelor party started, Paul called you and I overheard him telling you what you and he were going to be doing in Maui the following night." When his throat grew too tight, he stopped for a moment, remembering. "I hated myself for a lot of things that night in Boston," he said, giving her the rest. "But mostly I hated myself for the one brief second during that phone call when I wished him dead."

LAUREL DIDN'T SLEEP WELL that night. Exhausted, numb, she went to bed as soon as she got back to her room. But each time she started to drift off, she startled herself awake with a thought, a movement, a whimper.

She and Scott had had little to say—after having said

far too much—and she'd just wanted to escape. From him. From the things he'd said. From the different shadings he'd put on her memories of the past.

She didn't want him in there, messing with things she'd accepted long ago. Things she'd found places for.

She didn't want to feel things for him. Like desire. Romance. Love.

She didn't want him. And she did.

She'd needed to be alone.

At quarter after eleven, she reached for the phone, dialing by the light of the moon shining in the window of her second-floor room.

"Hello?" His voice sounded reassuringly normal. Far away, from another life, but something she recognized immediately.

"Hi."

"Laurel?"

"Yeah."

"God, honey, it's great to hear your voice."

"Yours, too. I didn't wake you, did I?"

"Of course not, I just got in a few minutes ago."

She'd known that. Shane was usually at the station until after the evening news.

"Where are you?" he asked, his eagerness flattering her battered heart. "Home?"

"No," she said, stretching beneath the covers, taking comfort in the sensation of the soft, cool sheets against her bare flesh. She'd neglected to buy a nightgown when she and Scott had gone shopping the other day. "I'm in Worcester. William Byrd's still missing, but we're finding all kinds of information. We're just not sure how it all fits together."

Shane talked to her for a while about the case, adding his own thoughts and suggestions, and though he came up with nothing she and Scott hadn't already covered, still it comforted Laurel. She and Shane had a lot in common.

"I miss you," he said.

"I know. I miss you, too." A lot, at the moment. She missed his predictability, knowing exactly where she stood with him. Shane had always been honest about the fact that he wanted her. That as soon as she gave the word, he'd have her in his bed.

"You don't know how glad I am to hear that."

Even while she smiled, a knot formed in her stomach. Maybe she shouldn't have called. "I think I have an idea," she said with a chuckle, one that was only a little bit forced. Shane was a very attractive man. Gorgeous, in fact. It wouldn't be a hardship to sleep with him.

"Have you made any decisions?"

"Maybe." She wanted to tell him yes, right then and there. That was why she'd called—to lock herself safely in with Shane once and for all. But she wasn't sure it would be for the right reasons.

She wasn't sure how she felt at that moment—except betrayed and confused.

And very, very scared.

CHAPTER FIFTEEN

IT HAD BEEN A WEEK. Maureen Cooper woke up Saturday morning with a heavy heart. When a child went missing, five hours was the mark after which officials started to consider abduction a possibility. One week of William Byrd missing was more than enough for Maureen to know that something was dreadfully wrong.

All of the rooms were rented for that weekend, with more bookings than they could handle coming in. But they'd had a couple of cancellations, too, after the article that got out about William's disappearance.

If something wasn't resolved soon, or if it was and the news was bad, the future of Twin Oaks was going to be in serious jeopardy.

But that was down the list of Maureen's concern. If any harm had come to William through Carl Nevil or his brother Owen, she was responsible.

And it wasn't just William. Cecilia Hamilton and Leslie Renwick were missing, too. And what about their other guests? And the twins? And Clint and Keegan?

Maureen had to pull herself out of bed. At times during the past week, she'd wondered if she was losing her mind. She couldn't focus. Couldn't do any of the things she normally just took for granted.

She thought she'd found the solution by leaving New York. Changing her name. Having her records sealed. Quitting the profession she'd loved.

Instead she'd become a sitting duck. And she wasn't sitting alone. She'd pulled a whole lot of innocent people up on the roost with her.

Maureen wasn't sure how long she was going to be able to keep still. She couldn't just wait around to be prey for Owen and Carl Nevil. She was a cop. A damn good one. She knew how to ferret out even the most obscure information.

If something didn't break soon, she was going to have to go back to work.

LAUREL DID WELL AT KEEPING up appearances—she'd had a lifetime of practice. Hiding from Scott was another matter entirely.

How could she pretend that what he'd told her didn't matter? How did she convince him that losing the image of the family unit she'd imagined herself a part of wasn't a big deal to her? How did she go back to not being vulnerable when he alone knew how vulnerable she really was?

Pulling on the undies and blouse she'd brought from Twin Oaks the evening before, zipping up the jeans, she felt completely naked. Exposed. She needed to hide from Scott. Yet he knew right where to find her. Literally and figuratively.

The Saturday newspaper was her solution for breakfast. Sitting across from him at the little coffee shop they'd found a couple of blocks from the motel, Laurel applied herself to the fact-filled print. She'd been a voracious reader of the news even back in high school, and since becoming an investigative reporter, she needed a newspaper in the morning more than she needed breakfast or coffee. Usually it helped her feel as though she was in control of all that was going on around her in her community, her state, her world. From weather to politics, she wanted a handle on it all.

But today the paper was also a hiding place.

"There's another West Nile virus scare," she read. "A couple more people have been infected."

"It can generally be treated, though," he said. Laurel heard his coffee cup land back on the table. He was on his second cup, but his bagel was sitting right where the waitress had left it.

He shared a few facts about the mosquitoes that carried the disease, but for once Laurel wasn't fascinated by his wealth of information. She was too busy trying to figure out how to act around him. She took a bite of her own poppy-seed bagel, though swallowing it past her dry throat almost choked her. She was going to keep up appearances, though. They were all she had at the moment.

"Did you sleep well last night?"

Laurel's skin burned. She couldn't talk about last night. She was barely able to think about it.

Lowering the paper a couple of inches, she peered at him over the top of it. His gaze was direct.

And lifeless.

Scott was asking for nothing. As far as he was concerned, everything was over.

She found she couldn't look away, but neither did she know what to say.

"Not too bad," she finally said.

She raised the paper. Now was the time for her to ask him how he'd slept. But she couldn't.

"I didn't get much sleep, either," he told her anyway.

She focused on her paper. Was he ever going to finish that coffee so they could get on with the business they were there to do?

To fill the awkward silence, she read him part of a story

from the crime desk. A young man had killed his pregnant wife because she was leaving him.

"It's a shame, you know?" she said, folding the paper and, dropping it on top of her unfinished bagel. "He not only killed his wife, but his baby, too. It's strange what people do supposedly out of love."

"Like winding up in a drunken stupor and getting your brother killed?"

She met his gaze. There was such suffering in those rich blue eyes, but all she could do was sit there while tears gathered in her own eyes and spilled over.

She didn't want to know that he'd been in love with her, or that he and Paul had broken their word to her.

She didn't want to know that he'd been blaming himself for his brother's death for three and a half years. Or what that guilt had done to him.

She didn't want any of it to be true. She didn't want him to be hurting and she didn't want to be hurting so much herself.

Yet she couldn't find any words to help either of them.

"We'd better go," Scott said. As he rose to his feet, his phone rang. Scott answered and pulled out his notebook. "Let me get that down," he said, scribbling what looked like a phone number to Laurel.

Laurel felt ashamed at the relief she felt when, judging by the rest of Scott's conversation, she knew they were going back to work.

"THAT WAS MURPHY," Scott told Laurel, pulling out his keys and donning sunglasses as he held the door for her and walked beside her to the Blazer.

"Has he heard from Dennis?"

"No." Scott's jaw was set. "Nor has Arnett shown up for work. At this point, when he does, he's fired."

"So what do you think our chances are of having him show up for his appointment with Murphy this afternoon?"

"Slim."

He wasn't surprised that she'd been thinking the same thing he had. But it made him damned uncomfortable. After unlocking her door, Scott walked around to his side of the Blazer. She shouldn't still be so much a part of him. Thinking like him. Touching him without ever lifting a finger.

"Murphy won't do anything officially until Arnett doesn't show, but he's checking hospitals for me," Scott told her after he'd climbed in and shut his door. He couldn't look at her. Couldn't stand to see the vacancy where once there'd been love in her eyes. Brotherly love, of course. "Arnett better hope he was in some kind of accident." Staring out the windshield, Scott tried to think like a con man would. "Or he better hope he never gets found."

Scott might not have grown up getting into trouble, being cared for by a rich older sister and brother-in-law, but he was pretty certain he could slip into Arnett's mind-set enough to know one thing.

The man was up to no good.

"I have to make another call before we start our rounds of the houses again," he said, beginning to dial. He had a hunch. And for once, it wasn't one Laurel would be sharing with him. The thought brought a mixture of relief and sorrow.

He was going to be spending the rest of his life not sharing with Laurel.

"Who are you calling?" she asked. "Does it have anything to do with that number you wrote down?"

He nodded, and then remembered that she wasn't looking at him, either. ''Murphy had someone search Arnett's phone records for me. There were a couple of numbers he couldn't easily identify.'' One had made the hair on the back of Scott's neck stand up. It was for a call last Saturday.

''Can't he get in trouble for that?''

''If he gets caught, maybe.''

''So what's noteworthy about this particular number?''

''It has a New York exchange.''

He pulled out his notebook, checked to make sure he had Frank Quigg's number right and hit Send. ''I might be way off, but I have a hunch...''

''And another favor to call in?''

Not this time. But Laurel didn't know about the connection between Dennis's prison friend and Maureen Cooper.

He gave her an apologetic look, which she missed, staring straight out the windshield as she was, and then said, ''Yeah, maybe.''

He'd only spoken with Maureen's old boss once, but the man remembered him immediately.

''I have an entire sheet of numbers in the Nevil file,'' Quigg told Scott when he explained his reason for calling. ''You want to hang on while I check, or have me call you back?''

''I'll hang on.''

''Wasn't Arnett's prison friend from New York?'' Laurel asked in the pause that followed.

Though he wasn't the least bit surprised she'd put things together so quickly, Scott was impressed. ''Yeah,'' he said, watching a woman park a pickup truck in a compact space.

He wished he could discuss his real concern about the Nevils with Laurel. And then was almost glad that he couldn't. Visions of William and Cecilia in the hands of either Nevil—even indirectly—were making him tense. He'd hate to think what it would do to her.

He glanced over at her, and she turned at the same time. "So you think there's a connection."

Their eyes met. And held.

Scott looked away first. "I'm just checking all bases."

He hated to lie to her again, even by omission.

Quigg came back on the line. "I've got a match."

Scott froze. It wasn't the answer he'd been prepared to hear. His lungs growing tighter by the second, he listened.

"It's the number of a woman Owen Nevil—Carl's brother—knows out on Long Island."

He'd hoped he was wrong.

"She's listed?" He could feel Laurel looking at him and braced himself for the conversation with her that was going to follow his phone call.

"No. Owen's been staying with the woman on and off since his release from prison. Several months ago she came to us asking for protection for her kid. She's got some rich uncle and Nevil wanted her to do a con job on the old guy to the tune of more than a million bucks. The jerk threatened to hurt her daughter if the woman didn't do as he asked. She begged us to take her kid someplace safe."

"Let me guess," Scott said, rubbing a taut hand across his forehead. "She wasn't willing to testify, right?"

"You got it."

"But you helped her get free of him. Watched out for her after she kicked him out."

"Yep."

"And then she let him move back in."

"You ever think about working for NYPD?" Quigg asked.

"Nope. Never…"

The day just kept getting better and better—and it was only morning.

"THERE'S A CONNECTION, isn't there?" Laurel broke the silence that fell after he ended the call. Though her seat belt was buckled, she'd slumped down so that her head barely rose above the dash. As though she were trying to hide from the truth.

"On the night that William and Cecilia disappeared, Dennis called a number where the brother of his prison friend was staying. Doesn't necessarily mean there's any connection between them and the disappearance of William and Cecilia."

"And Leslie."

"Right." Scott started the car, planning to do their daily drive-bys. He pulled onto the highway to head out to Dennis's place first. Leslie's was closer to town and he wanted to try to time their visit with Katy so that her daughters were down for their nap.

"The brother of Carl Nevil?"

Scott could feel her frustration almost as though it were his own. Hers seemed to be mixed with a bit of desperation, too.

Was it just the fate of William and Cecilia that concerned her? Or was something else sending her over the edge. Like him, maybe. Was it painful for her to spend time with him now that she knew the truth?

"Yeah—it's him." He told her about Owen's attempted blackmail of the woman he'd been living with.

She put one foot up on the dash, her arms wrapped around her middle. "That gives more weight to our theory that Dennis is blackmailing his sister, right? Maybe he took his cues from Owen." Her voice sounded strained.

Glancing over at Laurel, Scott worried about how much this was taking out of her.

And then told himself to get a grip. Laurel was an investigative reporter. She did this kind of stuff every day.

"Likely Dennis was nervous and checking in with the brother of his mentor for support for his own setup."

Whether Arnett or Nevil was behind this whole thing or not, Scott was becoming increasingly concerned for the fate of the three missing people.

LOOKING OUT HER WINDOW at the green-and-golden fields rushing by, Laurel tried to draw from nature's beauty to combat the dread flowing through her, but with no success.

You didn't work in New York news without knowing of the Nevil brothers. And while Laurel hadn't been in the business all that long, she'd been there long enough to know that if they were in any way connected to the three disappearances, their chances of finding William, Cecilia and Leslie alive were much slimmer. Especially since Cecilia had already given up the money.

Of course, she had a lot more to give, and Leslie apparently had an inheritance as well.

But it was unlikely Dennis was doing this job on his own. Arnett had never attempted a crime with such a high price tag either in dividend or penalty.

"Do you know any of the Nevils' history?" she asked Scott when her thoughts were growing too loud for her to keep them inside.

"Some." He sounded hesitant. Was he trying to protect her? "I know Murphy said they're big in the New York crime scene."

"Carl was one of the biggest until a little over a year ago. This female detective and her partner finally managed to nail him on more than minor charges. He's up for life. I followed Maureen Maguire's case from the beginning,'' she told him. ''She was an incredible detective.''

''How so?'' Scott asked.

''She was strong, confident, capable. And truly courageous to testify against him herself.''

''You're all of those things, you know,'' he said, slowing down because of traffic.

''I'm not any of those things.'' She'd been a coward her entire life. She would just sit quietly, melt into the background, make herself fit in.

''Laurel.''

She'd been staring out the side window, but turned at the commanding tone in his voice.

''You are strong,'' he told her. ''Your life has been extremely difficult but you've made the best of it—made a success of it. You're confident enough to know that you can do what you set your mind to. And, you are the most courageous woman I know.''

Maureen Maguire was courageous. She'd risked her life so that people she'd never even met could live more safely. Laurel lived her life in a little cubbyhole so no one could hurt her.

''You never had the security and unconditional love that most kids take for granted,'' Scott continued. ''You never had anyone believe in you, love you, simply because you were theirs, yet that didn't stop you from believing in love. In spite of a lifetime of rejection, you reached out when love came your way. You embraced it with everything you had. Most people would never have dared take that risk.''

Laurel could have argued with him, but he'd just made her feel good in a day that had been nothing but bad.

EVEN THOUGH THEY'D KNOCKED and found no one home at Dennis Arnett's house, neither Scott nor Laurel returned to the Blazer. Instead, they walked slowly around the premises, searching for anything they might have overlooked on their first visit.

"Let's go over here," Laurel said, heading toward the abandoned side of the building.

"Be careful, it's probably not safe." Scott followed her, though. It was unlikely they'd find anything; chances were good that Dennis Arnett had never even ventured over there, the place was in such bad shape.

Just as Scott suspected, the only thing they discovered was that the house was in sore need of renovation. Even the grass was dead. If he closed his eyes he could follow Laurel's progress around the yard by the sound of the dried grass crunching beneath her feet.

He saw her bend over and pick up something.

"What'd you find?" He walked over and peered over her shoulder. It was the closest he'd been to her all morning.

"Nothing," she told him, holding out what looked like part of a ring from a gumball machine.

She was right. It was nothing. The prize possession of some child who'd once played in this yard.

Obviously disappointed, she dropped the piece of toy jewelry back where she'd found it. Her finger was smeared with dirt.

Leaning forward, Scott took hold of her finger with the edge of his shirt, wiping it off.

He pretended not to notice when her knuckles brushed against his belly, though he didn't know whom he was pretending for. They'd both felt her fingers there.

"All clean," he said, backing away from her, glad she was willing to play along. They had to pretend there was nothing wrong between them. They had business to do. Much more important business than the two of them and their messed-up lives.

If he never breathed the scent of lilacs again as long as he lived, it would be fine with him. Standing there next to her, determined not to feel anything, he was damned pissed that lilacs even existed.

In that brief, awkward moment, Laurel looked at him. He could see the stress lines around her eyes and wished he had the right to soothe them. To ease her troubles.

He wished he had the right to do so much more.

After an almost silent trip out to Leslie's, they searched her yard, as well, keeping a careful distance from each other.

And when they found nothing, they crossed the street to see if Katy had any news for them. Scott's attempt to time things so that Katy's girls would still be asleep had failed. Within seconds of answering the door, Katy had both of them playing around her feet, making it very difficult for the adults to talk.

Not that Katy had anything new to tell them.

"I'm sorry," she said. "I think the girls are missing Leslie. Every time the doorbell rings, they think it's her. She's great with them and they're used to her being here for lunch fairly often."

The toddlers were attempting to play some rendition of dress-up—at least that was Scott's guess, based on the odd assortment of attire they were wearing—and when they started to fight over their accessories, a plastic bracelet specifically, he and Laurel excused themselves and left.

Scott couldn't remember ever being more happy to make an escape.

"WE NEVER HAD LUNCH." Laurel made the pronouncement as she climbed out of the Blazer back at the motel more than an hour later. Arnett had not shown up for his appointment with his parole officer, so Murphy was going to follow up on the hospital calls and check the morgue before he officially put out an APB on the man. He was going to call as soon as he'd done so. "Why don't I go for something while you go inside," she suggested. "You said you have some calls to make."

"That'd be great, thanks." Scott tossed her the keys, allowing himself a small, appreciative grin that he hoped she wouldn't notice. He wasn't used to having his thoughts anticipated. And no matter how good it felt, he wasn't going to get used to it. The domesticity of the whole thing struck him as ludicrous under the circumstances—yet oddly natural, too.

Laurel returned the grin, and Scott hurried inside.

He called Maureen immediately, and she took the news of Dennis's recent connection with the Nevils better than Scott had expected, especially in light of the fact that both Owen and Arnett appeared to be AWOL at the moment.

There was nothing to indicate that Owen Nevil was not on a hiking expedition as reported, she and Scott decided.

Scott could have been speaking with any number of his colleagues, if not for the hint of vulnerability in her tone. There was no doubt this was personal for Maureen. Her livelihood, her very life might depend on this case.

She asked if there was anything she could do. And then, as though thinking out loud, remembered her inability to do anything. She was an innkeeper, she told him. Nothing more. Scott had a feeling she was convincing herself more than him.

She still had her babies to keep safe, she reminded him. This scare had shown her that more clearly than ever before.

Just before ringing off, she begged Scott to keep her posted.

LAUREL PUT A BOWL OF chow mein in front of Scott where he sat at the table in his motel room, studying pages of notes, as though he didn't already have all the answers drumming through his mind.

"I'm sure we'll hear soon," she told him, wishing there was more she could do than push food at him that he probably didn't want any more than she did. It couldn't take Murphy that long to make his calls and write up the report.

Why couldn't they just go back a couple of days.

He glanced up and smiled, a weary yet warm and grateful smile. Laurel looked away. She didn't know this man—or the things he'd been thinking all those years when she'd loved him like a brother.

She had, hadn't she? Loved him like a brother?

Too upset to eat, too restless to do nothing, Laurel went over and washed her hands, then put a cool washcloth to her face.

"You still need to eat, even if you don't want to sit with me."

She jumped, dropping the washcloth. She hadn't heard him come up behind her with the water running.

"I…" How could she tell him that this motel room was far too small for a woman who hadn't been properly held for such a long time and a man who'd confessed he'd been lusting after her for eighteen years.

She took the bowl he held out to her, leaned back against the counter and started to eat, praying that the phone would ring and save her.

THE PHONE DIDN'T RING. And when the silence made the motel room almost more than she could bear, Laurel talked about the case.

"You know," she finally told Scott, "I've never even met Cecilia, and yet, after searching for her all these days, I feel really close to her."

She was surprised to see the frown on his face when he glanced her way. "Maybe that's because you were so fond of William…"

"What's wrong?" she asked him before she remembered her decision to steer clear of personal conversation.

"We might not get to her in time," he said gently.

"I know."

He gathered up their trash. "If you make it personal, it'll hurt like hell if we don't."

"I know."

"I don't want you to get hurt."

His words were soothing. Intimate.

"I know," she said again.

Scott would give his life rather than hurt her. She knew that instinctively. It was something that hadn't changed over the years.

And that mattered to her. It mattered a lot.

CHAPTER SIXTEEN

JUST A FEW MINUTES after four o'clock, Officer Bill Murphy called Scott to tell him that Dennis Arnett was dead. They'd just identified him today when Murphy went down to the morgue. Dennis had been on his way to the airport, flying under a false identification, which was why they hadn't been able to find next of kin.

"What?" Laurel cried when she heard the news. Sinking down to the bed, she stared up at Scott. "How? When?"

"Last Sunday afternoon." Scott's tone was as grave as the look in his eyes. "He was killed in a car accident going to the airport. He'd reserved a seat on a flight to Bermuda. They found almost a million dollars in a suitcase on the seat beside him."

"What about William and Cecilia? And Leslie?"

He leaned back against the dresser, his feet crossed in front of him, his arms folded. "Nothing."

All this effort. All this time. And nothing. Laurel couldn't believe it.

"They're pretty sure he was trying to make a call when he crashed," Scott added. "The officer on the scene cited the cell phone still clutched in Dennis's hand as the cause of the accident. Witnesses said Dennis hadn't been paying attention to his driving and missed the shuttle bus coming up in the lane he was merging into."

"Was anyone else hurt?"

Scott shook his head.

"I wonder who he was calling?"

"Murphy's number was still on the phone's LED readout," Scott said.

"You think he was going to tell him he was leaving town?"

"Or maybe tell someone where his sister is…"

Laurel was so frustrated—and frightened—she had to fight tears.

Dennis Arnett had been fleeing the country with a fortune of his sister's money. And Cecilia, William and Arnett's girlfriend, Leslie, were still nowhere to be found.

Even after all life had shown her, Laurel still found it shocking. It all seemed so pointless.

She got up and walked over to gaze out the window until she had herself better under control. Eventually she turned to face Scott.

He hadn't moved.

"So what do you think?"

He watched her for a long time, just looking into her eyes, into her. "I don't know what to think," he said softly.

And Laurel knew suddenly that he wasn't just talking about William and Cecilia and Leslie.

He didn't know what to think about her. And him.

She didn't know, either.

"I need you to be my friend," she whispered.

"Always."

She had no idea what she and Scott could ever be to each other, or even if they would stay in touch beyond this time. All she knew was at this moment, she needed him.

DAMN. SCOTT HATED the helplessness that washed over him.

He didn't know what to do to take the stricken look from Laurel's beautiful gray eyes. Didn't know how to help William and Cecilia. Couldn't even find out if they still needed his help.

And Leslie.

"She could still have them," he said suddenly, straightening from the dresser to face Laurel.

"Who?"

"Leslie. If she and Dennis were partners, she could still be holding Cecilia and William someplace."

"I don't…"

"Think about it," he said, almost giddy with the surge of adrenaline pumping through him. "She could have been the next person Dennis was going to call, and when the call didn't come, she wouldn't know what to do. She's a technical writer, not a criminal."

"At least not until she fell in love with her own uncle."

Scott cringed. "We don't know for certain that he was her uncle."

"We don't know anything for certain," Laurel reminded him.

"Suppose William and Cecilia are still alive somewhere, that Dennis was holing them up someplace while he made sure he could access the money he'd made Cecilia transfer and then get his butt out of the country. He probably had Leslie stay with them until he was certain that Cecilia had done what she'd said at the bank and he had the money in hand. It's possible that Leslie had been told to wait for his call and then meet him at the airport. And when the call didn't come, she was stuck with two kidnap victims on her hands."

"He only had one plane ticket," Laurel objected.

"Maybe she had her own. On the other hand, do you think he'd really plan to take her?"

"No."

"So, to follow this through..."

"He could have been calling Murphy to tell him where to find William and Cecilia and then maybe he'd been planning to call Leslie so she'd get the hell out of there," Laurel finished for him.

"Yes." There was a particular feeling Scott got when he was finally making things fall into place. He was pretty sure he was getting that feeling now.

Of course, it could just have been the fact that he and Laurel were working together again as one unit. Not two separate entities who just happened to be traveling along an identical road.

He watched her pace around the room. Loved the grace with which she moved. Loved...

Something was teasing Scott's mind. Slumping into the chair he'd vacated earlier, he pulled out his notebook and flipped through the pages, hoping to trigger whatever was escaping him.

There were pages and pages of stuff. None of it good. Worse, nothing was clicking.

His gut like rock, Scott read on, anyway.

"I'd forgotten Maureen had run into Dennis in Cooper's Corner." Laurel's voice was hushed behind him, giving him chills. Or perhaps it was the words scrolling in front of him that were doing that.

He hadn't known she was behind him. Laying the notebook in the middle of the table, he turned it so that, if she sat in the other chair, they could both see it.

Once she was seated, Scott forced himself to relax, to allow the thoughts to flow so everything could fall naturally into place.

Another, not completely related thought struck him, and it was one he couldn't share with Laurel. He was fairly certain, based both on instinct and the fact that things were so tidy without Owen Nevil's involvement, that the New York criminal had nothing to do with William Byrd's disappearance. It didn't seem like the Nevil brothers to let another man, one with as little kidnapping experience as Dennis, handle a job with such a high payout. And that would let Maureen completely off the hook—except that Dennis had seen her.

What if he'd also seen a picture of Maureen, Carl Nevil's nemesis, while hanging out with Nevil in prison? It was highly likely that if Carl intended to put a price on her head, he'd be showing her picture to people. Especially someone who might be getting out soon and could help him keep an eye out...

And if Dennis knew the Nevils were looking for Maureen, if he recognized her that day in Cooper's Corner, that phone call to Owen Nevil might have some very serious implications.

REACHING THE LAST PAGE of the notebook, Scott read the notes he'd jotted after their walk around Dennis's house.

"I know where they are." Finally.

Scott was so relieved, he almost felt good for a second. Laurel was staring at him. "Where?"

"Remember that piece of ring you found today?" he asked, pictures flashing through his mind.

"Yeah?"

"Didn't it strike you as odd that it wasn't any dirtier?"

"I don't know. I guess."

"It's obviously been a long time since any kids lived there, so whatever child might have lost that ring during play would have had to lose it a long time ago."

"Unless it was a neighbor kid."

Maybe. But he didn't think so.

"Remember that bracelet the Miller kids were fighting over today?"

"Oh, my God!" Laurel jumped up and grabbed her purse. "It was the same kind of plastic jewelry."

"Katy said Leslie plays with the kids all the time. That ring must have fallen from her pocket, or her purse. Maybe she dropped her purse." Yeah. That sounded more likely to him.

"They're at Dennis's," Laurel said, waiting by the door as Scott collected his keys.

"Or at least they've been there," Scott said. He looked up at her. "My guess is they're locked somewhere in the abandoned side of that house...."

OTHER THAN THE QUICK phone call Scott made to Murphy, tense silence filled the Blazer. Although Laurel found it uncomfortable, small talk was impossible. Thoughts of what they might find—two older people locked up without food or water for a full week—were too frightening.

"I didn't see that ring in the yard today," Scott finally said. "Good work."

"Hurry, please?"

"Of course," Scott said, pushing a little harder on the gas. "You know, I'm wondering if maybe Leslie was an innocent pawn in all of this, as well," he said. "Maybe she dropped that ring on purpose, to let someone know where they were."

"Maybe." Laurel liked the sound of that. "It would certainly make more sense. Otherwise, where has she been all this time?"

"Running? Hiding? Scared to death?"

"Or she could be coming late at night to bring food

and essentials and is just keeping them there until she can figure out what else to do."

It could have been any of the above.

"Don't worry," Scott said in response to Laurel's heavy sigh when he finally exited the highway. "We'll find them."

He wasn't looking at her, but he reached across to take Laurel's hand where it rested on the console between them.

She wrapped her fingers around his, gathering up his warmth and the innate goodness that had compelled her to be near him all the years she'd known him.

Until she remembered him telling her why he'd been responsible for Paul's death.

Feeling guilty as hell for liking the feel of his strong male hand wrapped around hers, Laurel slid her fingers away, folding her hands in her lap.

SCOTT STOPPED THE BLAZER in front of the partially renovated house. Murphy knew the landlord and was bringing a key to both sides of the house.

That instinct that he'd learned to respect when he was still too young to understand what it meant had taken over. With complete confidence, he followed where it led.

The end was coming. There was no longer any doubt.

He just wasn't sure which end. For Cecilia and William? For Leslie? For him and Laurel? For all of them?

Once they reached the house, he had to stop himself from suggesting—begging—that Laurel stay in the Blazer. He wanted her safe. And if Leslie was still there...

If she was holding William and Cecilia hostage...

He had no right to dictate Laurel's life.

"Remember, if it gets dangerous, you do exactly as I

say,'' he instructed, more for his own benefit than because he had any doubts about her.

''Of course.''

''Here's Murphy.''

Getting out of the Blazer, they both watched the police car pull into the drive. At Scott's request, Murphy accompanied them inside. There still was no police investigation, no evidence other than an accidental death and hunches put together, no crime committed.

As they entered the unrenovated side of the house Arnett had been calling home for the past month, following behind Murphy, Scott grabbed Laurel's hand.

She fell so naturally into step, taking his lead without hesitation.

She might not respect him anymore, but she still trusted him.

In all likelihood that trust was going to be the last thing she ever gave him.

Inside, the house was as bad as he'd expected. Plaster hung from the walls, and there were gaping holes in the floor. It smelled like someone had forgotten to take out the trash. With the windows boarded up, the front room was dark and gloomy as they slowly picked their way behind Murphy.

The police officer told them the landlord had described a boiler room in the basement that had cement walls and no windows. They were going to check there first.

''Please, God, let them be okay,'' Laurel whispered. Her breath tickled the back of his neck.

She was so close to him he felt her words like impressions in his mind rather than heard the sound. He felt her desperation. It was as though they were one, creeping stealthily through the night. One being. One body. One energy.

If determination could make things happen, they would get William and Cecilia out of this mess alive.

Unless they were already too late—a possibility he couldn't ignore.

He didn't respond, except to squeeze the hand he held. As much as he hated taking her into whatever hell lay ahead, he was glad to be sharing this with her. To be making this memory.

Assuming it turned out well.

It had to turn out well.

As they neared the basement stairs, Scott felt a tug on his hand. "Scott?"

Murphy started down the stairs without them as Scott turned, his face almost touching hers.

"If anything happens down there…"

He shook his head, holding her gaze in the shadowy house. Because the light was so dim, he wasn't certain what he read in her expression. Wasn't sure he wanted to know.

So he was not at all prepared when her mouth moved closer.

Caught completely by surprise, Scott opened his lips to hers, taking hungrily what she seemed to be offering him. The urgency of the moment left no time for gentle coaxing. For asking—or waiting for an answer. His tongue met hers ardently, demanding and giving in equal fervor. Her taste was still so new to him, and yet his body felt right at home, connected to hers.

"Laurel," he whispered. There was so much he needed to say, yet he knew it had already been said.

She shook her head and reached up to kiss him one last time. A soft, lingering kiss. Without a hint of passion.

The impact of that gesture shook Scott more than anything that had gone before. The air left his lungs, and for one crazy second he wondered if he could take another step, go on to do the job that awaited him.

Taking his hand, Laurel positioned herself behind him again, ready to face the future—the one that had become defined in those short moments.

He might not yet know the fate of William and Cecilia, but he knew his own. Laurel had just said goodbye.

Pulling her close once more, Scott positioned his mouth just over her left ear. "I'm going down alone," he said. "You stay up here."

"But…"

"Please, Laurel. Just until we know that Leslie isn't down there holding a gun on them. Worrying about you will be a distraction."

Especially now, when he was one vacant ache inside where she was concerned.

He waited for her nod, and then, before he did something stupid like kiss her goodbye, he left her.

LAUREL WAITED, BUT ONLY UNTIL she heard Scott reach the bottom of the stairs. Then she followed him. She hadn't come this far to stop now.

Conscious of Scott's peace of mind, she hung back, making certain that he didn't know she was there. If something went wrong, if Leslie was in there armed, they needed someone to be able to call a backup crew.

As the men neared the boiler room, Scott reached out and tapped Murphy on the shoulder. Laurel couldn't hear what was said, but the officer stood back and let him go first.

The reality of the situation was all too clear to Laurel. If someone was inside that door with a gun, Scott could be walking straight to his death.

No!

The reaction was instant.

I love him, God! Laurel's mind screamed silently. *He can't die. I love him.* She'd never known she could cry inside. Never known something could hurt so much.

She'd thought losing Paul had been the worst thing that would ever happen to her. Now she wasn't so sure.

Heart pounding so loud she was afraid it was going to give her away, Laurel watched as Scott took a tool from Murphy and worked on the brand-new lock she'd only just noticed on the boiler room door. Murphy held a small flashlight for him.

Please let him be okay. The prayer mingled with the one her heart had been whispering since they'd first started this journey a week ago. *Please let them be okay.*

The lock gave way, and Scott swung the door open.

Laurel held her breath as he stood poised in the doorway.

"There!" The urgency in Murphy's voice sent chills through Laurel. She could no longer stay put as both men disappeared inside. Just as she reached the door, she heard a moan. Relief flooded through her. Someone in that room was alive.

CHAPTER SEVENTEEN

THE MAN WAS LYING up against a wall. At first glance Scott thought he was dead—thought they were both dead. The woman was spooned up against him, her head on his shoulder. But as he got closer, he could see the faint rise and fall of both chests.

They were breathing.

While Murphy checked out the rest of the small room, Scott approached the sleeping couple. William was the first to wake, his face immediately filling with alarm as he automatically pulled Cecilia beneath him, shielding her. Still mostly unconscious, she moaned at the rough treatment.

"It's okay, William," Scott said softly. "We're police officers, here to help you."

"Oh." The older gentleman slowly sat up, pulling Cecilia with him.

"What?" the woman cried out in fear and confusion.

Leaning down to her, William said, "Shh. It's okay, my love." He looked up at Scott. "They're here to help." The older man's voice broke and tears filled his eyes.

"Help?" Cecilia asked, still obviously dazed.

"We're saved," William said. "We're saved."

"Saved?" Seemingly unaware of the other people in the room, Cecilia stared up at William. "Are you sure?"

William smiled at her and nodded, then turned her face toward Scott. "See?"

"Oh." The woman looked, blinked, and looked again. "Thank God," she whispered, and then started to cry.

Murphy stood beside Scott, both of them grinning.

Then William looked behind Scott as though something else caught his attention.

"Laurel? Is that you, child? Or am I dreaming things again?"

"It's me, William," Laurel said, coming forward. She was crying, too. And as much as Scott knew he should be mad at her for not following his orders, he was inordinately pleased she was there.

She needed this. Deserved it. He couldn't believe, after all she'd been through with him this week, she was still there, believing in happily-ever-after. She was the strongest woman he'd ever known.

Yet when he met her eyes briefly, there was a longing in them. He foolishly, briefly took hope, thinking that it was for him.

On her knees, with one arm around each of them, she hugged William and Cecilia. "I'm so glad we finally found you," she said, her voice heavy with emotion. "Glad that you waited for us."

Murphy said he was going to call the paramedics, and then, when the captives had had a couple more minutes to orientate themselves, Laurel helped both of them to their feet. After a week in captivity, William and Cecilia were weak, and Scott stepped forward to help, but Laurel took their weight as though they were rag dolls.

Cecilia was a slender woman, dressed in what must have been a very elegant and expensive dress when she'd put it on the week before. Her silver hair was now completely matted to her head.

William's suit was torn and wrinkled, his face stubbly

with a week's growth of beard. What little hair he had was sticking straight out.

As Scott watched Laurel help the couple stand, he knew he'd been wrong about that longing look.

Laurel was a professional. Capable. Strong.

She didn't need him.

IT WAS A LITTLE LATE for introductions, but as they stood together in the boiler room that had been home to the couple for an entire week, William introduced Cecilia to Laurel, who, in turn, introduced Scott.

"So how long's it been since you've had anything to eat or drink?" Scott asked. Laurel was relieved when he moved forward to help shoulder the weight of the older couple.

"I think it's only been dark under the door once since we finished off the last of the bread and fruit that bastard left us," William said. "There's still a little water, but only because we've been rationing so carefully."

Cecilia cringed and started to cry, burying her face against William.

"You're talking about Dennis Arnett," Scott said.

"Cici's little brother, yes," the author said, and there was no doubting the bitterness he felt toward the man.

Scott figured the news of Arnett's death could wait awhile.

"By the way, do you have any idea how long we've been here?" William asked, frowning.

"Today's Saturday. You've been missing a week."

Cecilia still shaky, but steadier than she had been, turned to Scott. "Our daughter's here," she said, her gaze focusing as though she were only now coming to her senses.

"*Your* daughter?" Laurel and Scott asked at once.

"Yes, *our* daughter," Cecilia said. "I wish I'd had the courage to say that thirty-five years ago." Her eyes filled with tears again.

"Shh, you promised," William said softly, his eyes earnest as he looked down at Cecilia. "We aren't going to waste time going backward."

Scott and Laurel exchanged a glance that warmed Scott in places he'd grown accustomed to being cold. They might have hit on the hiding spot correctly, but there were obviously some other things they'd had grossly wrong.

William was a father. And any fool could see there was no way this man was blackmailing this woman.

"When we got Dennis's letter with the picture of him and Leslie together, we knew we had to get to her as soon as possible to tell her the truth," Cecilia said. "She couldn't date her uncle."

"But when we got there, Dennis was waiting for us with a gun," William said. "We didn't have a chance. He'd already taken Leslie away."

Scott could feel Laurel's closeness as he asked, "Where'd he take her?"

"Here," Cecilia said. "He'd been on his way to New Ashford to find out why, after all the pressure he'd applied, I wasn't calling him. He was driving through Cooper's Corner and saw William and me together. He said he couldn't take a chance on us getting to Leslie, she was his backup ace, so he went to her place and forced her to leave with him. He locked her up and then went back to Leslie's to wait for us. He knew we'd come."

The woman seemed to wilt from the effort the long speech cost her.

"Leslie's locked somewhere close by," William interjected. "Up until it got dark the last time, we'd been calling out to each other. The first couple of days we talked a lot—she was almost as thrilled to find us as we were to finally find her. She said she'd been looking for us for a couple of years, but kept reaching dead ends. Anyway, as the days wore on and we had less and less to drink, we decided not to talk as much to keep our throats from getting so dry and sore. The last day or so we only talked enough to make sure we were all okay and to promise one another to hang on. The last time we called out to her, there wasn't an answer.''

"She's probably asleep," Cecilia said. "That happened a couple of times before when she didn't answer."

"Do you have any idea where she is?" Scott asked. He had to force himself to be patient, to remind himself that Cecilia and William were light-headed, suffering from disorientation, hunger, shock, and probably completely unable to feel any urgency.

"In a room next door," Cecilia said.

Laurel looked at Scott, brow raised. "I don't think there is a room next door. This is the basement."

"It might not be right next door," Cecilia said, her voice growing stronger. "But she's close."

It only took Scott a couple of minutes to locate a small traplike door just outside the boiler room that appeared to be some kind of closet. It took another couple of minutes to get the door open.

The young woman huddled in a ball on the floor woke up instantly when light flooded into her cell. She'd managed to fashion a bowl of sorts out of what looked like some kind of tin, half filled with water. As she stood, she stepped in it, tipping it over.

"Thank God," she said. "I exercised every day—rationed the food the bastard left me. He said he'd call Murphy to come get us as soon as he got to the airport but I gotta tell ya, I was starting to lose hope...."

At that she burst into tears.

With a strength Scott could only marvel at, Cecilia pushed her way through to Leslie and, for what had to be the first time in her life, held her daughter in her arms. Looking at Cecilia, he could easily believe that she was never going to let go again.

Scott had been fairly stoic up until that point. But when he saw William join his two girls and heard Leslie sobbingly ask if everything they'd told her that past week was true and not just some dream to get her to hold on, and then heard William tearfully tell her yes, even Scott choked up.

Somehow Laurel was there then, sliding her arm through his, pressing against his side as together they watched one family get a happy ending.

THINGS WERE CHAOTIC after that. The paramedics arrived and Leslie convinced her parents to allow themselves to be strapped to the gurneys just long enough to be carried up the stairs. She won their agreement only when she promised to stay right there with them. And then they were all on their way to the hospital for checkups and probably rehydration IVs.

It wasn't until a couple of hours later, in a private hospital room that now had two beds, that Scott and Laurel finally heard the whole story. After filling out reports at the police station and checking out of the motel, they stopped by the hospital on their way back to Cooper's Corner. They stood together, though carefully not touching, at the end of Cecilia's bed. Once she'd received the older couple's permission, Laurel switched on her tape recorder.

Just as they'd guessed, Dennis had come to Cecilia for money when he was released from prison. What he hadn't known was that after years of buying him out of every scrape, William Sr. had made Cecilia promise that she would never give him another dime of their money, even after his death. He did it to protect Cecilia. He knew he wasn't going to be around forever and knew, too, that Dennis would take everything Cecilia had if he could.

"When Dennis seemed to calmly accept my decision, I was overjoyed," Cecilia said. She was propped up in bed against a pile of pillows. William was sitting on Cecilia's bed, holding her hand.

Scott envied them that familiarity. Laurel's fingers were only inches from his—he could practically feel them there—yet she suddenly felt so off-limits they might as well have been on different continents. Was it only hours ago that she'd kissed him?

Kissed him goodbye.

"I thought prison had finally done what my husband and I and all of my love could never seem to do," Cecilia was saying. "Mature him. It never even occurred to me, when I got a copy of Leslie's birth certificate with her adoptive parents' names blocked out that Dennis was behind it."

Scott could have told her that some men never change. Or mature. After all these years, all the guilt and grief, the confession and rejection, he was still in love with his older brother's woman.

"You thought it was from William," Laurel guessed.

"Yes." Cecilia nodded. "I thought he'd crossed out the Renwicks' names because he and I were Leslie's parents. I thought it was an olive branch. I'd sent him a note a couple of years before telling him his father had passed on, and I just thought it had taken him that long to forgive me for marrying his dad."

"You knew William before you married Mr. Hamilton?" Laurel asked.

"Oh, yes," Cecilia said, exchanging another look with William. "I was in love with him."

"But you married his father."

Laurel's voice held no censure, only a nonjudgmental encouragement to Cecilia to tell her story. Scott was impressed. If circumstances were different, he'd have saved the thought to mention to her later.

"Dennis was in trouble," Cecilia said. "I'd gotten him a job at Hamilton Lending and he'd stolen from the company. He was only sixteen. William's dad threatened to press charges unless I married him."

"My father was not a very compassionate man," William said, his voice less forgiving than it had been moments ago. "He knew what he wanted and how to go after it." And then, obviously shaking off distasteful memories, he continued his story. "A few weeks ago, when Cici called me and told me we had to meet, I thought she was the one offering the olive branch. I knew if I met her, it could appear that I was really after my inheritance."

"He wanted our first meeting to be in private, so he had me come to Twin Oaks after everyone left for the barbecue. He had the negligee I'd forgotten in his hotel room the night that Leslie was conceived," Cecilia said, blushing. But that didn't stop her from leaning over to give her lover a soft, albeit long, kiss.

Scott felt more than heard Laurel's sigh beside him. He couldn't help but wonder if, after all was said and done, he'd have a moment alone with Laurel, a chance to say goodbye to her in private before they all went their separate ways. Would she let him take her back to Cooper's Corner?

Or would she fly straight to New York and arrange to have her car sent?

More to give the older couple a moment to recover than anything else, he glanced over at Laurel. She looked back at him, and he ached at the uncertain emotions he read there. He'd never meant to hurt her. Disillusion her.

He'd only ever wanted to love her.

LAUREL WATCHED AS Leslie Renwick, dressed in a hospital gown and robe, came into the room a few minutes later and sat at the end of her mother's bed. She hadn't needed an IV, but they were still keeping her overnight for observation. She'd showered and her short dark hair was fashionably mussed, her gamin features healthy looking.

Somberly, Scott told the threesome about Dennis's death. William held Cecilia while she cried softly, but, though she was sad, she said she hoped that he'd finally made it to a place where he could feel loved and be happy.

Laurel wasn't sure how all that worked, but she hoped Cecilia was right.

As quickly as she could without seeming insensitive, she guided the conversation back to the story she had everyone's permission to write. She was eager to get the facts she needed and leave these people to their privacy.

It seemed that while Dennis had just been intending to blackmail his sister, whiting out the Renwicks' names on the birth certificate as a warning to her that he knew the truth, he'd unknowingly brought two lifelong lovers together after a thirty-five-year separation. It didn't take Cecilia and William long to figure out who'd really sent it. Cecilia had thought that William was the only one who knew she'd given birth to his baby three years after she'd married his father, William Hamilton Sr. But William knew one other person who had that knowledge, because he'd shared it with Dennis himself. He'd confessed that he and Cecilia had finally lost the battle against their growing love and had one night of passion neither of them would ever forget. William had hoped that his frankness would shock the kid into taking care of his own troubles, finding a way to pay his own debts, to set Cecilia free to marry William and raise her daughter.

Of course, Dennis had simply let Cecilia continue to take care of him and lose herself in the process.

So, telling her aging husband that she was accompanying her alcoholic mother to a clinic and rehab center in Iowa for six months, Cecilia had gone off to have her baby. She'd kept in touch with William Sr. by phone the entire time, and together she and William Jr. arranged the private adoption of their daughter, giving her to Hamilton Lending's wealthiest, but also despairingly childless, clients, Robert and Gloria Renwick. Cecilia had never met the couple personally, but she knew of their reputation through their business dealings with Hamilton Lending. She had no reason to believe she'd ever come in contact with her daughter as the Renwicks lived in another town. And, as it turned out, she never had.

"That was when I finally told my father I was quitting the family business," William said. "Of course he disowned me, which I'd always known he would. I left then and moved to Connecticut, where I was able to do the things that I love—travel and write books."

"And I grew up with a great set of parents," Leslie said, her eyes misting as they met Laurel's. "Unfortunately they were killed by a drunk driver a little over five years ago."

"I'm so sorry," Laurel said, feeling much more than

she could possibly express. Never had she had such trouble keeping the personal and professional separate.

"So what about Dennis?" she asked softly, trying to keep things on track so she could finish her job and leave these good people alone. Scott shifted beside and Laurel tried to ignore the small jump her nerves took. "I'm imagining you cared for him a lot?"

"My brother told us that he'd only dated Leslie as a bargaining chip." Cecilia interrupted, sounding almost like a protective mother hen as she answered for her daughter. "Thank goodness he didn't try anything with her."

"My folks and I talked a lot about Dennis that first day we were in captivity," Leslie said, her eyes meeting Laurel's. "I still can't believe I was so gullible, so easily duped, but I can't be sorry I knew him when it brought me my parents...."

Her voice trailed off, and Laurel knew the other woman was going to have some recovery to do emotionally as well as physically, but she was completely certain that Leslie would have all the emotional support she needed to learn to trust herself again. Laurel looked at Scott, wondering if he'd ever know that same peace. He was looking right back at her, his gaze resigned.

She couldn't bear the emptiness she saw there.

"The picture in your travel book on the nightstand," Laurel asked William quickly, reminding herself why she was there. "Was that of you and Cecilia?"

"You saw that?"

"When you went missing I took everything in to be fingerprinted." Scott didn't sound as if he was having any emotional struggle at all. "Your computer's at the county precinct office as well, safely locked up."

"Thank you for that, young man," William said.

"When things got too..." He glanced at Cecilia. "Well, anyway, we left my room at Twin Oaks and went into town for something to eat and to finish our discussion. When Cici told me about telling Dennis he wasn't getting any more money from her, I knew he was up to no good. She hadn't been home in a week so I suggested we go out to her place to see if there was any more communication from him. We stopped back at Twin Oaks to pick up my stuff, but the lock was stuck and the key wouldn't work. When we got to Cecilia's, we found the letter with the picture of Leslie and Dennis together. I never gave my computer another thought after that. You know, I think this is the first time since I got it that I haven't worried about losing the material inside it."

Laurel shifted, her shoulder accidentally touching Scott's. She hated how obvious her quick move away must have been. "Maybe because you've got something that matters more now?"

"Most definitely." The older man's voice trembled with emotion. "And yes, that photo was of me and Cici, taken the last time I was in Boston before she left to have Leslie...."

William had what mattered more than his career. It was something Laurel wanted more than anything else in life.

CHAPTER EIGHTEEN

AT A ROADSIDE REST STOP an hour later, while waiting for Laurel to come back from the ladies' room, Scott took the opportunity to phone Maureen. He and Laurel had both called earlier to tell Maureen the good news about William and Cecilia, and Scott had been waiting for a chance to call back and reassure Maureen that the Nevils were not in any way involved in the kidnapping.

He was surprised when the ex-cop wasn't immediately relieved.

"Frank Quigg called this evening," she told Scott in the impassive tone of one who was distancing herself from reality. "He had a letter for me there, addressed to my married name."

Watching for Laurel in the darkness, Scott braced himself. "You had him open it?" he asked.

"Yeah, it was only one line—'You can't hide from me. I will find you.'"

IN THE WEE HOURS OF THE next morning, Scott pulled into the drive at Twin Oaks.

"Funny, isn't it," Laurel said as the Blazer came to a stop in the yard. "Cecilia thinks she made the wrong choice, giving up her baby. And my mother made the wrong choice keeping me."

She couldn't remember ever being so exhausted, and yet she felt strangely on edge, as well. Something more had to happen. The day couldn't end yet, whether the clock said it had or not.

"I guess it just goes to show there are no absolutes. No clear-cut rights or wrongs."

"You have to take each situation, look at the people, the circumstances," Laurel added.

"I guess."

He grew strangely quiet. She wondered if he was as beat as she was.

In a way Laurel was grateful for the numbing fatigue that consumed her. This way she didn't have to think about what lay ahead.

"I know it's late, but would you mind coming up for a few minutes?" Laurel asked.

Butterflies swarmed in her belly. Face burning, she stared straight ahead as Scott pulled around to a parking place close to the door.

"I…"

"Scott," she interrupted, needing to be direct. "We have to talk. I know we're tired, but now seems like a good time. You don't have to stay long."

She almost crossed her fingers when she said that.

Taking a shaky breath, she issued one last prayer for the evening—a prayer for the right words, a clear understanding, and the assurance that whatever happened, it would be the best thing for both of them.

SCOTT STOOD JUST INSIDE the door to her room. He couldn't remember a time when he'd felt so awkward. He didn't know what they had to talk about. Hadn't it all been said? He wondered if Maureen was sleeping somewhere in the house, or lying in the dark worrying herself sick.

He'd bet she was asleep. The woman hadn't made it through years with the NYPD without being tough.

"Have a seat," Laurel said, pulling off her sandals and plopping down on the end of the bed. "It's hurting my neck to look up at you."

He sat down on a wooden bench at the end of the bed.

Laurel took a deep, almost dramatic breath. "Okay," she said, folding her hands and dropping them in her lap. With her makeup long gone, her hair wind-tossed and shoved behind both ears, she looked about sixteen and ready to give him a speech he was going to disagree with.

Scott braced himself.

"First, the other night... You threw a lot of shocking stuff at me all at once...."

"I'm sorry."

She looked up from her feet long enough to glare at him. "You have no reason to be sorry, and it would best if you'd just let me get through this—the first part, at least."

Thankful to be relieved of any responsibility in the conversation, Scott nodded.

"Okay, as I was saying, you threw a lot of things at me. There was no way I had a chance to grasp it all—to have any idea what to think until I'd had time to sift through it."

She was going to give him the lashing he deserved. He couldn't blame her.

"So now that I've had time to think, there are a few things I have to say...."

She paused and looked up, her brow raised in question.

It couldn't be anything he hadn't already told himself, though coming from her it could turn out to be more painful.

He nodded for her to continue.

She was nervous. He could have done without the tenderness that welled up inside him.

"The seat belt thing." She was looking straight at him. Scott would have preferred her to continue studying her feet. The top of her head was easier to take. "You were planning to drive that car."

He said "Yeah" only when she made it obvious she wasn't going to continue without a response.

"Paul didn't take any risks you weren't already taking yourself."

"Laurel…" he started to argue.

"Because you didn't consider it a risk at all," she continued.

"I knew about the recall notice, he didn't."

"But you also believed the risk was nonexistent. I know you, Scott. If you'd thought there was any danger, you wouldn't have let Paul drive that car no matter how drunk you were."

He couldn't argue with that. Not that it absolved him of the responsibility.

"And just as we learned from Cecilia's decision to give up Leslie—it's the motivation that counts."

She'd caught him between the eyes and he hadn't seen it coming. "But…"

"No buts this time, Scott. I'm right and I'm not letting you talk me into anything else. You are not to blame for the fact that Paul was thrown from that car. Period."

He couldn't let go that easily. But she had an interesting point about motivation.

She was quiet, as though waiting to see if Scott was going to argue, and then continued.

"Second, Paul driving."

He reinforced the walls he'd built. She wasn't going to

talk him out of that one. He was going to be accountable for the rest of his life.

"Paul was a grown man with the right to make his own choices. You are neither responsible for nor answerable to those choices."

"I..."

"You were drunk and I'm surprised and disappointed about that," Laurel said.

He wasn't going to let the weight of her words crush him. He'd known they were coming.

"But Paul had been drinking, too. And he was the one who decided to drive, whether he was hungover or not. You didn't say, but knowing your older brother, I'm quite certain he intended to drive whether you were in the car or not."

He vaguely remembered some kind of threat along those lines.

"And knowing you, there'd be no way you'd let him tackle that feat alone."

When had she come to know him so well? It had always been Paul for her.

This was the oddest dressing-down he'd ever had. She was listing all of his crimes—though he cringed when he thought of the one to come—and yet, she wasn't doing nearly as good a job as he did in making him feel like a scum.

"Your point?"

"The accident was just that. An accident."

Scott sat there, fingers forming a steeple against his chin. He could feel his skin getting tight. Hot.

He must be more tired than he'd thought. He almost felt lighter. As though the weight that he bore every day was giving him an hour off.

For that he'd gladly never sleep again.

"Now, the third thing—the way you say you felt about me."

"The way I *know* I felt about you." The look he sent her was ruthlessly piercing. She wasn't going to make pretty with this.

Her shoulders slightly hunched, she glanced down. Oddly enough, she seemed more embarrassed than disgusted.

"Yes, well, the fact is, you can't help how you feel, Scott. I mean, if we could choose who we love, lots of us would choose differently. Heck, I'd have chosen to fall in love long before Paul if I'd had any way to make it happen."

He stared at her.

"I'd have done it again since, too, rather than be so lonely these last three and a half horrid years."

He couldn't find the hole in that argument, either.

"What matters is what you did with the feeling," she continued. "The only thing you could control was the response you chose, not the emotion itself."

He wished she'd just yell at him and let him get out of there, drive home and sleep it off in the familiarity of his own bed. Or maybe he'd just sit up in his Blazer all night. That was a hell of a lot closer, and the front seats tilted back far enough.

Hell, he could even bum a pillow off her. And maybe a blanket. Not that he'd need one. He was always warm. But the late summer nights were getting cooler.

"Scott?"

She'd moved over to the edge of the bed, her feet touching the floor. "Yeah?"

"The point is you didn't make a wrong choice," she said. "Falling in love was something you had no say over, and your response to that was everything you could ever have hoped it would be. You were honorable. Loyal to both your brother and me, but also to yourself. You did nothing to be ashamed of. You never once acted on your feelings. As a matter of fact,'' she chuckled, though with little mirth, ''I was completely blown away the other night. All that time we spent together and I never had one hint that you felt anything for me except affectionate irritation.''

Slow down. Stop the train.

He had to get off.

Somehow between doing his job that night and ending up in this room, he'd gotten on the wrong ride. He had no idea where he was or where he was supposed to be, for that matter.

''Scott, are you listening to me?''

He nodded. Of course he was. To every word. But...

''You really think all that stuff?'' he asked.

''I know it,'' she said. Her conviction was damned hard to fight.

''I knew it the other night, Scott,'' she said, dropping to the floor. She was on her knees at his feet.

Scott didn't know what to do about it.

''I was just so shocked that I didn't know what to say, what to tackle first.''

He'd give just about anything to believe that.

''And,'' she added, interrupting his thoughts, ''because I was scared to death.''

''Scared?'' That was news to him.

''I was scared because when you told me you used to be in love with me, all I could feel was this crushing disappointment that I hadn't known—and that you no longer felt that way.''

What?

She reached forward and buried her face in his knees.

"Because that was the moment when I realized that I'm in love with you. Not with Paul's memory. Not with the idea of you as family, but with you, the man who questions everything. And knows the answers. The man who would give his life for those around him. Who never gets tired of fighting the good fight. The one who accepts the worst the world has to offer, and can still see the beauty, too. The one who is so loyal he puts his brother's happiness before his own. Who is so honorable that, out of respect for his brother's memory, he doesn't speak up for himself even when he has a chance at a happiness of his own...."

He swallowed. Or tried to. His throat was so dry he could hardly breathe.

"And that realization scared you," he said, his voice sounding as though he hadn't used it in years.

"To death. How could I love you and not be disloyal to Paul?"

Exactly.

"And then it hit me, Scott. I'm not the same person I was all those years ago. Paul's death showed me that absolutely nothing is a sure thing. All my life I'd thought it was my circumstances that made life seem so uncertain. But the truth is, life *is* unpredictable. Even Paul—reliable and loyal as he was—ended up leaving me alone."

He didn't know what to say.

"I don't know how long I'd have run scared if not for tonight," she said.

"What happened tonight?"

"William and Cecilia. That vow they made. The one William reminded Cecilia to keep. To not waste the future on things of the past. I suddenly realized that's exactly what I was doing. I will always love my memories of Paul, but life has changed me."

"And what does the new Laurel need?" Scott asked.

"You," she said, looking him straight in the eye. "I need you."

He'd always known that Laurel was a miracle. An angel sent from heaven to save the Hunter men. He'd never known, until that moment, that she was sent to save him.

Once that was made clear to Scott, he didn't continue to question it to death. There would be more talk, more searching and analyzing. He knew that. It was his way. But he'd seen the light.

That was enough.

"And I need you," he whispered, an unfamiliar moisture gathering in his eyes. "I love you, Laurel. God knows, I've never stopped...."

With an energy he shouldn't have had, Scott pulled Laurel up off her knees and into his arms. He drew her against his heart, where, he promised the fates, he would keep her forever, cherishing with his very life the gift they'd sent him.

Laying her back on that big four-poster bed, Scott started to undress her slowly, his fingers trembling as they reached the buttons on her shirt. He'd never known such desire.

"I can't believe it's really you," he whispered, leaning down to give her a long, convincing kiss. Convincing to him.

"It's me," she said. "And you, Scott. Me and you. I think a part of me has always known it was meant to be this way."

Scott stopped and looked at her by the dim light of the bedside lamp. "You don't mean that."

"I do," she said, and there was no doubting the conviction in her eyes. "You understand me," she said. "We've always thought alike...."

"Yeah."

"It kind of felt like we were meant to be together, you know?"

Scott could die right then and go to heaven a happy man. But because the fates allowed him to remain, he stripped off the rest of Laurel's clothes quickly, before they reconsidered.

"You are everything I imagined you to be, and more," he told her softly, reverently as he stared down at her nakedness.

"You're embarrassing me." She made no attempt to cover herself up, though.

"You love it," he told her.

Her "Oh, yeah" sent him over the edge.

Scott kicked off his shoes, then stepped out of his pants and pulled off his shirt at the same time. He turned off the light and joined her on the bed, knowing firsthand what ecstasy meant as he felt her naked body against his own.

And then, as naturally as if they'd been doing so for years, her body opened to his, inviting him in, and Scott pushed himself into heaven.

"I love you," he whispered as the first thrust took him deep inside her.

"I love you, too. Always," she whispered, looking him straight in the eye as his body rocked in and out of her.

She was really his.

It was the last coherent thought he had that night.

LAUREL AND SCOTT MADE IT downstairs before breakfast the next morning.

In between the lovemaking during what was left of the night, a lot of decisions had been made.

Laurel was going back to New York, but only long

enough to turn in her story, quit her job and make the necessary arrangements to vacate her apartment and move her things to Cooper's Corner.

And say goodbye to Shane.

He was a good man and deserved to have a woman love him as completely as Laurel loved Scott.

Maureen was outside playing ball with the twins, keeping them occupied, while Clint put the finishing touches on breakfast. Seeing Scott and Laurel, Maureen called to the girls to play by themselves for a minute, then ran across to the couple.

"Thank you." she said, pulling Laurel into her arms. "I'm so relieved everyone's okay."

Laurel hugged the other woman back without any of the usual reticence she felt when being touched. She wondered if it was possible to be too full, to have dreams come true too much.

And decided that she was willing to spend the rest of her life trying to find out.

Keegan came around from the back and snagged the twins up, screaming and kicking playfully, one under each arm.

"I assumed when I saw your Blazer still here this morning that you two finally figured out you were meant for each other," Maureen said softly.

"Yeah," Laurel and Scott said, looking at each other lovingly. Laurel couldn't help but remember just the night before when she'd been so envious of a similar look shared by William and Cecilia.

She thought of Leslie. The thirty-five-year-old woman was proof somehow that adopted kids could belong. Even if their birth parents made mistakes, they weren't destined to be unwanted. It was something Laurel had needed so badly to believe.

In that second, with Scott's arms around her and her new friend smiling on, Laurel's heart was completely filled with the miracle of love for the first time in her life. And once felt, she knew it was something she'd never be without again.

She had a home. A man who loved her. Friends who would share life's ups and downs.

She belonged.

*   *   *   *   *

Welcome to Twin Oaks—
the new B and B in Cooper's Corner.
Some come for pleasure,
others for passion—
and one to set things straight...

COOPER'S CORNER
a new Harlequin continuity series
continues in September 2002 with
AFTER DARKE
by Heather MacAllister

When small-town plumber Bonnie Cooper visited New York in search of vintage bath fixtures for the Twin Oaks B and B, her reputation as the Berkshires' Blind Date Queen followed her. But an arranged dinner with city-bred columnist Jaron Darke went from bad to worse when they witnessed a mob hit outside the restaurant. They had no choice but to hide out at Twin Oaks. Their cover...they're engaged!

Here's a preview!

CHAPTER ONE

"I HAVE HAD ENOUGH of New York, thank you very much." Bonnie had had enough of everything at this point. She stood and picked up her purse—which had been searched earlier. "Goodbye."

As she walked toward the door, she half expected Jaron or Quigg to stop her, but they didn't.

That could have been because the door was locked. "The door is locked," she said without turning around.

"She's from *very* far out of town," Jaron said.

Bonnie marched back to the table. "Why are we being treated like prisoners? We have cooperated fully. You have everything you need to know, and I want to go home—or back to my aunt's apartment, then home. And I want to go *now*."

"No can do." Quigg didn't look sorry, either.

What was it with men ignoring her requests all of a sudden?

"You're going to be guests of the city of New York tonight. Maybe several nights."

Oh, no, she wasn't. "Nice try, but just call me a cab and I'll consider us even."

Quigg laughed.

Jaron looked at her pityingly.

The door opened and one of the detective duo stuck his head in. "One bed or two?"

Quigg glanced at them. "Two. Did you really have to ask?"

The detective held up two fingers to someone, then nodded at the captain. "All set."

"Good work." Quigg was once more all business. "Okay, listen up."

Bonnie listened, but she didn't like what she heard. "You've got to be kidding." She'd said it before and she'd probably say it again. Captain Quigg actually wanted to keep them in protective custody.

"For how long?" she asked. "I've got a renovation I'm due to start on Monday."

"As long as it takes."

"You've got to be kidding."

"No, Bonnie, he's not kidding, so you can stop saying that."

Bonnie ignored Jaron. He'd done nothing but glare at her, and make derisive remarks for hours. Well, she was *glad* she'd seen this side of him. Yes, Jaron had now revealed himself in all his sarcastic glory. Her first impression of him had been right on the money. Oh, for a time there during dinner she'd thought he wasn't so bad. Rub away that cool exterior and there was a gleam of an attractive man beneath. Actually, the man on the outside wasn't too bad, but she was going to ignore that. She would even have been willing to tolerate another date if Aunt Cokie had insisted on it, but not now. Uh-uh. No way. The sooner she got away from him, the better.

And then the Cooper's Corner Blind Date Queen was going to turn in her crown.

"So, how long *do* you think it'll be until we're free to go?" Jaron asked.

"We'll need a positive ID on Sonny O'Brien. But firs

we've got to find him. And until then, we're going to keep you two under lock and key.''

''*We* are not the criminals here!'' Bonnie couldn't believe this was happening. ''You can't do that.''

''I can and I will.'' Quigg laced his fingers together and leaned forward, looking up from under those bushy brows. His voice was deadly earnest. ''We have been after McDormand for years—even before we knew who he was. Before we knew he existed. You've seen our only picture. The man is like a ghost. And now he's slipped up, and you two are the best chance we've ever had of getting to the guy. If you think I will jeopardize that chance, then you are very much mistaken.''

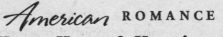
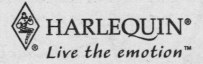

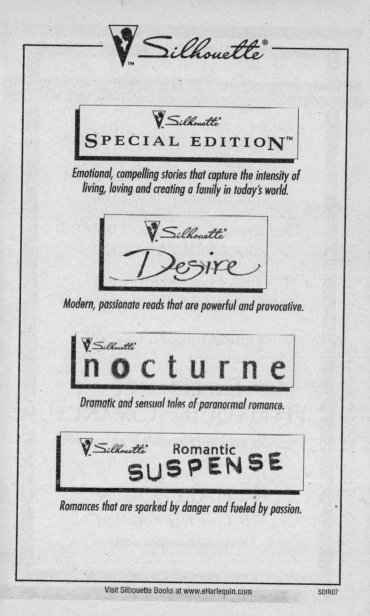

Silhouette®

SPECIAL EDITION™

Emotional, compelling stories that capture the intensity of living, loving and creating a family in today's world.

Silhouette® Desire

Modern, passionate reads that are powerful and provocative.

Silhouette® nocturne

Dramatic and sensual tales of paranormal romance.

Silhouette® Romantic SUSPENSE

Romances that are sparked by danger and fueled by passion.

SDIR07

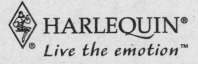